THE ONE WHO SET OUT TO STUDY FEAR

The One Who Set Out to Study Fear

Peter Redgrove

BLOOMSBURY

First published 1989
Copyright © 1989 by Peter Redgrove

Bloomsbury Publishing Ltd, 2 Soho Square, London W1V 5DE

British Library Cataloguing in Publication Data
Redgrove, Peter, *1932*
The One Who Set Out to Study Fear
823′914 [F]

ISBN 0 7475 0187 4

Six of these stories are adapted from
radio plays which were originally
broadcast on Radio 3 in 1987.

Grateful acknowledgment is made for permission to
reprint lines from *The Poems* by Dylan Thomas,
published by J. M. Dent.

Drawings by Jeff Fisher
Photoset by Rowland Phototypesetting Ltd,
Bury St Edmunds, Suffolk
Printed in Great Britain by Butler and Tanner Ltd,
Frome and London

'Over the centuries,' says Peter Redgrove of the stories collected in Grimm, 'they have drawn new details to themselves, like magnets attracting iron filings. They have become a sort of tuning device to the magic world.'

Peter Redgrove gives to the re-telling of each story its own pace and a manner suitable for the present day. Each is lovingly and appreciatively rooted in the original, but cast in an individual and energetic style that is both disrespectful and enchanting. Redgrove finds the predicted, the unpredictable, the frightening and yet also the necessary. Funny, sexy, sharply-observed, set in a world where the magical and the contemporary marry, commenting one upon the other, these stories come into that rare and special category that makes us say, Oh yes, of course, I knew that . . . but I'd forgotten it until now.

Peter Redgrove is the author of numerous volumes of poetry and the classic work *The Wise Wound*, written with his partner, Penelope Shuttle. He is a widely respected novelist and playwright: his affirmative analysis of our uncommon alternative senses and the 'amorous science' of human life, *The Black Goddess and the Sixth Sense*, was published in 1987. Most of these stories first appeared on the BBC as radio plays.

CONTENTS

The One Who Set Out
to Study Fear

The One Who Set Out to Study Fear

'Father, what is fear? Are you afraid, Father, why are you shuddering?' Sonny is at his father's deathbed. The cottage room is stifling hot. Sonny is fascinated at the way his father's heart-beat shakes his chest, bared for the physician.

'Quick, bring some water. Sponge his brow,' says Mother. The sick man is streaming with a pungent sweat. The heat in the room seems to come from his body.

'I think you had better go, Sonny. Our father is very ill,' says Greg, his elder brother, a large sombre presence.

'But . . .' Sonny has never seen death, and he wants to stay. Greg is studying for the ministry, so has professional rights. He's older than Sonny, too.

'Let him stay. He loves his father.' Greg shrugs. Mother will have her way.

'Mother, why is Father shuddering?' asks Sonny.

'My dear, he's dying.'

'Is he afraid of dying?'

'Dear, your father is almost in the other world.'

'He's nearly gone,' whispers Greg.

Sonny is puzzled. 'Then there's nothing left but a shudder on the bed. Where is my dad then?' There is a great shudder and sigh from

3

the dying man. Sonny leans across and breathes it right in, holds his breath as if to savour his father's last syllable.

'Now he's in the other world.' Mother has not noticed Sonny's catching her husband's last breath.

'When I go there, will I shudder too?' These words are made of the dead man's breath. Mother starts to weep. Greg looks at Sonny, appalled.

It's a year since the funeral. Uncle has come to supper with his sister. He is a gravedigger. It is a cold night and he has an appetite after his day's work. He is a wiry man in his sixties. He leans back in his chair, picking his teeth and regarding Sonny with curiosity.

'They tell me, boy, that you're quite fearless.'

'Yes, Uncle. I just seem to get interested when the other boys get frightened.'

'I call that exceptional.' Uncle doesn't believe a word of it. 'What are you going to be when you grow up?'

'A surgeon maybe. Most people are frightened of guts.' Sonny ponders. 'Or maybe a parapsychologist,' he says, with a delighted little smile.

'Yer what?'

'A man who studies ghosts and hauntings scientifically and without fear.'

Uncle wants to teach the boy a lesson. 'You'll need experience either way. Graveyards is holy places and the bones guard God's house. I'll make you my apprentice so by the time you're ready for the university you'll know bones and ghosties inside out.'

'Are you fearless, Uncle?'

'Nothing scares me, Sonny. I've been a gravedigger man and boy fifty years, and I've never seen anything to shudder at.'

Sonny perks up. He can learn from this man.

'But, Uncle, when I looked out of my window last night I saw you on your way back from the inn leaning on the corner of the house and shuddering and throwing up . . .'

Mother interrupts. 'I think apprenticeship is a very good idea, Sonny, whatever you do after. Brother, I'll give you fifty pounds and he can be indentured to you.'

'Sixty.'

'Fifty's what his father left him.'

'Done.'

'Uncle, don't you fear God then?'

'No, boy. He lives in that church, which I helped build with my own hands. If God had built it, I would fear him.'

'I'm like you, Uncle. I'm not afraid.'

'Aren't you, my boy. Then you can start with me at cock-crow tomorrow.'

Sonny finds the work enthralling. That people can be made of so many different pieces! They have worked all day, and Uncle is explaining the current job.

'God's acre is full to bursting. We've got to pack the skellies of the old 'uns neatly. They've got to go into the church crypt. It'll make the church holier, our prayers more powerful. Just dig down, Sonny, and when you find a skull put it in this pile. Split timbers in this pile. Long bones in this. Ribs and little bones here. Vicar reckons we can burn most of the body-bones and the old 'uns won't be too upset. It's the skulls and long bones we've got to keep. The names went long ago. This is good work. I love to sit on the edge of my pit with a good pile of skulls on my right hand and long bones on my left, munching my sandwiches, listening to the hours pass, tolled out by the church clock. Reckon I'll get on to my tea now, Sonny.'

It is nearly dark. Sonny stands with a skull in his hand, like Hamlet.

'I'll work on a bit, if you don't mind, Uncle.' He smiles back at the skull, gently.

The work absorbs him. He goes on digging and sorting, sorting and digging, oblivious of the tolling hours. He has been given a key to the church, and starts carrying bundles of bones like pale harvest sheaves into the crypt. His uncle is of course furious with him. If the lad works like this, then there will be no work for anyone else to do, and they'll both be out of a job. It is his fearlessness and his curiosity which make him work so hard, so if he gets a fright he'll be a bit more careful. There is a bright moon, and from his cottage window Uncle can see the glow from the pit in the churchyard where Sonny is still working with his Tilly lamp. Uncle opens a press and takes out the musty shroud in which Sonny's father, his brother-in-law, was buried. It is an exceptionally fine one, made of silk with lace frogging down the front. Uncle stole it from the coffin because it was so fine, but as it is instantly recognisable he has not been able to sell it yet. Occasionally he sleeps in it, as the sweet-slippery silk helps him masturbate. He goes to the scullery to fetch the skull he has whitewashed and the little black wickerwork wastepaper basket, the bottom of which he carefully cuts out with the saw on his pocketknife. The skull is quite dry, and he fastens it to the top of the wickerwork cylinder with raffia. Then he goes back to the bedroom and in the long mirror tries on the headpiece. It is in effect a black wicker mask he can see through, surmounted with a gleaming white skull. Now he fastens the shroud to the wickerwork at his chin and neck and lets it fall about his body. The illusion is complete. Uncle himself finds it quite frightening. There is Sonny's father in his unmistakable burial clothes with his bare and radiant skull floating a little above the high neck of his lacy shroud. Uncle pulls the headpiece off and takes a pull at his bottle.

Sonny at last has nearly finished. He dowses the Tilly lamp and climbs out of his pit. A cloud slides over the moon and he is aware in the sudden darkness of a white figure standing at the edge of the excavation regarding him silently through black holes in a skull floating like the moon and as radiant white. He is surprised, and deeply interested. The possibility of a deception does not enter his innocent mind. The apparition is as profoundly interesting as the whole day in the churchyard has been, and a fitting climax to the day's work.

'Father?' he says, 'Is that you? Are you in the next world, and is it this one, the graveyard?' He steps towards the ghost, which takes a slight step backwards, then recovers itself.

Mark me.

I will.

My hour is almost come,
When I to sulph'rous and tormenting flames
Must render up myself.

Sonny has read that this is how ghosts talk. It is deeply interesting. *Geistsprache*. His memory is equal to the occasion and he feels it right that there should be a formal language in use. Besides, he wants to keep his father there. What secrets he can learn by questioning him!

'List, list, O list!

If thou didst ever thy dear father love . . .' groans the ghost, and Sonny replies, ardently, walking firmly towards the horror, arms outstretched.

'Haste me to know't,' the boy cries, 'that I with wings as swift/As meditation or the thoughts of love,/May sweep to my revenge . . .' and with a high thin cry the ghost disappears into the pit.

Sonny is amazed. Something capable of floating a skull should not fall into ordinary holes. The moon comes out and he can see how his uncle lies in the pit shuddering and foaming at the mouth. A jagged long bone pierces his chest. A final shudder, and he lies still. Sonny lights the Tilly and clambers down. The headpiece with the skull fastened to it is lying by the body. The deception is plain. But mere deception is not interesting. With a gentle smile Sonny closes his uncle's staring eyes. So greatly did this old man love his brother-in-law, and the graveyard ghosts of which he was now one, that he sought to become him, and by ritual disguise to penetrate the secrets of death. It was a holy play and a mummer's mask. But clearly the police must be fetched. They should not be allowed to trample all over this holy act with their big boots. And the news must be broken to his sister. Anybody might stumble into a grave with a few drinks taken. Carefully Sonny unfastens the raffia that holds the skull. Now it is just another bone face and a bit of an old basket. He pulls at the shroud; the silk slips easily off the body, and it is just an old man lying dead in his working clothes. Sonny can make out the outline of a flask in the front pocket of Uncle's overalls. Without haste he takes it out and sprinkles its contents over the corpse's chest. Then he folds up his father's shroud, puts it in his pocket, and goes home to bed.

Sonny got his place easily, and started reading for the medical Tripos. Girls at Cambridge were in short supply, but he was never short of at least one hanger-on, fascinated by his glitter and refusal to shudder at even the most gruesome medical curiosities. He liked to use the girls as a lay audience. One day Diana remarked: 'I just think it's a beastly habit to eat your sandwiches in the dissecting-room, Sonny.'

'Hold this a moment, lover,' said Sonny, suddenly busy. Diana shrieked and hopped as the voltage went through her. Sonny was delighted.

'Bastard,' said she.

'Don't you feel better for a little galvanism from the electrical machine?' was his response.

'The shudder went all over me, everywhere.'

'Were you afraid? Let me feel your pulse. It's fast, slowing now.'

Diana began to sigh.

'It feels good now, like after a cold plunge. That was very naughty of you, Sonny.'

'It makes people shudder. It'll make the corpses shudder. But shuddering is not fear. I attach the terminals to this dead man, half-dissected, his breastbone wide open. The heart hops, the teeth click and the eyes roll. Yet it has no pulse. Do you believe in ghosts?'

'Look here, Sonny, I love you and all that, but you have made yourself very disgusting with your experiments.'

'I believe in ghosts. I think they are made of electricity and perfume. How can one be frightened of that!'

'I can't tell whether you are a saint or a mad scientist. Sonny, let's go to bed.'

'No, I don't want to. I'm too busy. Look at this cadaver hanging on the rail. Apply electricity and the hair stands on end and it starts dancing.'

'Don't you want to go to the disco then?'

'No, the smell's terrible. I love the pungent formalin smell of this place. And if I want to, I've got somebody to dance with.' It is a pallid freckled dead adolescent, break-dancing on its rail.

'You're simply horrid.'

'I know,' said Sonny. Diana slammed the door. He didn't really care whether she was there or not. He went on talking to himself.

'The dead can't shudder and no more can I, but surely I'm as alive as anybody. My pulse – it's completely steady and regular whatever happens. How can I shudder if my heart does not shudder, if my pulse is always the same? I think people shudder when they think of dead folk. They call any place they are buried holy, and this is the same as "haunted". Everybody is worried that being afraid of the dead will create that shuddering electricity which brings them to life. I think by fear and shuddering people raise ghosts. Or what they call ghosts. Thus I am ideally suited for my vocation of parapsychologist, since I do not shudder, and under all circumstances I remain cool. So I am in command and can observe what is happening around me. But I have my mystical side, I am capable of belief, though I am not capable of shuddering. I remember how surprised the lads of the village were when they found me in the church at midnight not long after that episode of my uncle falling into the pit. Anyway, those lads knew I liked to hold vigil among the dead 'uns who live behind "they pretty marbles", as my uncle used to say, and they too wanted to frighten me and then hustle me into the duckpond. What they did not know was that my practice was to stand in front of the altar with my eyes open and my arms stretched wide, echoing the figure on the cross. I could go into a kind of aware trance in this position, for hours if need be, but I was listening. I found by experience that if I stood in the right place and remained utterly silent I could gradually pick out in the echoing-chamber of the chancel my own heart-beat which built up around me in the darkness an echo the exact size and shape of the church. In sounding its shape out of my own heart-beat, I became the church. Prayers and hymns moved inside me. It is a wonderful experience to dream you are a building. The only time I ever felt afraid, just a touch, in the midnight church, was when for a moment I thought I detected another heart-beat behind one of "they pretty marbles". But it must have been an extra little echo inside the space of the tomb. Yes, those lads were so confused to find me standing like that when they burst in that they were unable to catch me for my ducking. It seemed that I passed among them and they could not lay a hand upon me.'

Sonny was already mildly famous when he sought out Princess Raskolnikoff in her handkerchief factory.

'Excuse me, Princess. You won't know me, but in my way I'm almost as famous as you are.'

'Famous. What for? For not working? For owning a haunted house? For being the fag-end of a Tsarist line and called Princess? For being glum? For never smiling? For being unworried? For being in charge of my absent father's handkerchief factory? Who let you in?'

'You could be a most beautiful woman.'

'An air of paralysed glumness is never attractive. Or I hope not.'

'Please. I would call it an air of mystery. The television programme said you would marry anyone who cleared your dower-house of haunting atmospheres.'

'Is that what you call them?'

'I have always found that so-called ghosts have a natural explanation. Bad drains, for example, make bad dreams.'

'I have seen an army of zombies flowing down the stairs ready to engulf and eat me. One caught me by the ear. Do you see this ragged stump I keep under my hair? Is that proof enough?'

'Nevertheless. We experience such visions through the psyche. Their power and horror is a measure of our repressions. If you refrain from fear, they become conversable. Many people go into violent involuntary shudders when they see a ghost, catch at their clothes, may even tear an ear.'

'OK. What's your reaction to ghosts, wise guy?'

'I never shudder. Whatever the ghost looks like, however frightening, I converse.'

'With bad smells?'

'Or with holographic projections arising from piezo-electricity in the walls raised by the coherent vibration or shudder over the house-tops of a wind prevailing at certain times of the year; the so-called ghostly anniversaries. I have several theories.'

'I can see that.'

'Whatever the reason, you can tune yourself to these appearances by adopting a friendly, bluff attitude, not being scared, and asking the right questions. Maybe of yourself.'

'The conditions are clear. My father's instructions lay down that whoever makes the house habitable may own not only the house, but also the income from the estate, and me into the bargain. My last suitor could not get out quick enough, and hanged himself in the front hall instead. The one before that decapitated himself when he flung himself out of a first-floor window without opening it first.'

'I should posit naturally occurring LSD vaporised from an underground spring, and give myself belladonna injections as an antidote to the drug beforehand.'

'You try it then. Here's the key, the address and a map. But, just a sec. What experience do you actually have? You talk a lot.'

'I am a professional parapsychologist. Call me Sonny. I am a scientist. A scientist of the strange. I uncovered the practical joker who was the sooty dog of Meacham Manor, the rapist hound.'

'*That* scientist of the strange! Oh well . . .'

'And I solved the mystery of the screaming door in the hills . . .'

In the car on the way to the haunted mansion, Sonny kept up his accustomed soliloquy.

'As I enter Princess Raskolnikoff's park, it is an unrolling panorama, like the painted rolls of scenery on a Victorian pantomime stage, where animals possess the wisdom, and all transforms to mental opulence at the end. These trees in their avenues, how haunted my headlights make them seem, as though snipped out of paper, as though fretworked out of cardboard, as though engraved on steel. It is like the contents of the mind unreeling at the day's end, the "Hades bobbin bound in mummy-cloth". Yet that is how things are, the tormented ghosts of each day line up for inspection. I expected owls . . . Whoo-hoo old howler, like a winged face rushing towards me in the headlights. The avenues like gallows trees in endless bobbing procession, gallows trees whose roots have drunk up and become intoxicated by the balsams exuded by torments of their victims, and dance in the wind like struggling criminals reborn, with waving emaciated arms, with bulging knotted eyes, with big bellies soft as bread with rot, with rainy sweat and tossing foliage dead on the branches, for if such were not so palpably evil, would they not die less meanly, and with fewer struggles? Yet these are reflection of my own soul, which, somewhere far off, must be shuddering.

'A gravel parterre, a house rising with its mansards against the moon. Mandible Towers, at last. I can get my equipment out. Will Tombs the butler be waiting for me? No, I must heft my own luggage. A complete ghost hunter's apparatus – designed to encourage a conversation with any phantom. Microphones, oscilloscopes, infra-red cameras, all the gear. If my instruments register a presence, if their readings convince me of the reality of an appearance, then I know I am not wasting time talking to myself. A slinky shadow – the place is inhabited, if only by cats. Somebody puts the milk out for them, and I nearly stepped on the saucers. Now, the Rumkorf coil, to give me plenty of light. Where shall I camp for the night? A library. Good. Next, a sewing-room, walls brocaded with a pattern like those anguished trees of the driveway. What's this great door? Oh – I nearly shuddered then – a chapel and the altar served by white shapes, a congregation of white shapes. Well, I suppose you have to shroud your private chapel with sheets to keep the dust off, like anywhere else . . .

'Now the kitchen. Big table. Big old cold ranges. I'll make my headquarters here, for the first night, anyway. The cats have followed me in . . . here they come, three fine black cats. Hello Princess Cat! You have two fine Nubian consorts. I have the cats to talk to. They know all the secrets of this house, no doubt, and how they may be purged. If I can let them enter my fantasy, then we shall converse together, and I will learn what I need from the subliminal sensoria of my imagination or from the deeper levels of my own psyche, no matter. In short, I shall pretend the cats can talk, since there don't seem to be any ghosts around at present. What else are cats for? You seem to be hungry. No, that's *my* sandwich. Well, in the best tradition of the fairy tales, I will share it with you, not be stand-offish. Stand-offishness will get me nowhere, even though I am constitutionally unable to pay a ghost the compliment of being afraid of it. The cats will share my meal and this communion between man and animal will be like a favourable initiatory dream ensuring safe passage through the night.'

'On behalf of myself and my two toms, I thank you,' said the largest of the three black cats.

'There! I nearly shuddered again.'

'If you're afraid, we won't be able to communicate. Most of your kind are afraid all the time.'

'I could have sworn that cat talked. It's a good thing I cannot feel fear.'

'Would you like a game of cards – whist or gin rummy?'

'Oh, whist. There are four of us here. That makes a good game. Cut for trumps. Let's make this a bit more interesting.'

'I never play for money.'

'How about souls?'

'Our souls against yours?'

'Done. I'm feeling lucky tonight.'

'We'll see. Shall we say our souls in the form of nice fat herrings?'

'Why not. I see you have everything prepared. A dish appears on the kitchen table. Four nice kippered herrings. Winner eats all, I suppose.'

'That's it. Before the night is done I shall be licking you from my whiskers.'

The princess arrived next morning to find Sonny staring at one of the machines.

'I like watching the folding-machine, particularly the part where it shakes the hanky before ironing it neatly. The machine reminds me of a cage of butterflies. Or a houseful of ghosts.'

'What happened? At least, you're here this morning, not hanging throttled in one of my closets.'

'I told you, no ghost can destroy the man who is prepared to converse with it. I use the term ghost tentatively, to include imaginary figments.'

'Does that include God?'

'What else is prayer but celestial conversation? I used to pray by offering my echoed heart-beats in church, when I was a younger lad and my senses were even sharper than they are now.'

'You can't be more than twenty-four.'

'True. But each science has its season. I woke up and there was a plate of three delicious kippers. I had them for breakfast. Thank you.'

'I didn't bring them.'

'Then I must accept the interpretation my waking dream put on the house. It says the fishes I ate were the souls of three powerful were-cats.'

'Then you have got their power by eating their souls for breakfast. That makes me shudder with joy. Perhaps together we're throwing off this burden. Maybe we will one day marry, our hearts beat as one.'

'If I have gained cat-nature, that will not help me shudder. Cats don't shudder, they glide.'

'You have two more nights to go in Murder Manor,' said the princess, firmly.

Sonny believed that soliloquy was the clue to self-friendship.

'I'll try the chapel tonight. Let me try the church experiment again with my own heart-beat. See whether I can still do it. These sheeted pews make me shudder – almost. If I am very still I can hear my heart-beat echoing from the ceiling, the floor, the organ pipes. But there's some other sound here. A faint singing. A singing like church. Hymns are being sung somewhere in this house. Somewhere. Here! Here. Where? Is the organ somehow vibrating to buried waters? Is it like a crystal radio decoding in its tin pipes the VHF of late-night Radio 3, or even the audio of TV? I'll whisk the sheet off the organ. No, just an old organ. Wait! The keys are playing themselves. Very faintly. That's the music – where are the voices coming from? Here, let's get the sheet off the cross and the altar. Ah, the voices are louder. Now off the pulpit. Why, there is a minister in it, with his hymn book, singing lustily but ghostily. Now, sheets off the choir pews and the congregation pews! Why, they're full! A complete chapel choir and congregation singing "Lead, Kindly Light". What fun. I will join in. It's the least I can do.

> *'Lead, kindly light, amid the encircling gloom,*
> *Lead Thou me on,*
> *The night is dark, and I am far from home . . .*

'But what a strange-looking bunch they are. All carrying some implement. There's a big man with a scythe, and his brother next to him has got a pitchfork. There's their mother with a rolling-pin, and daughter has got a big cleaver. Father must have come straight from chopping wood. Everybody is holding some murderous instrument or other. What is this homicidal Christian community? All their eyes are

13

turning towards me now with a vile pallor in them, as though they
needed blood. And their hymn?

> *'Just as I am, without one plea*
> *But that Thy blood was shed for me,*
> *And that Thou bidd'st me come to Thee* . . .

'Not bloody likely. They are out to get me. Well, I will sing on,
fresh hymns, hymn upon hymn. They can't murder me while we are
singing together. I was right, brows murderously frowning, now they've
stopped singing, they are making their way out of the pews into the
aisle. The choirmaster is a rough-looking customer with his chainsaw.
Quick – another hymn. "Rock of Ages".

> *'Rock of ages, cleft for me,*
> *Let me hide myself in Thee;*
> *Let the water and the blood* . . .

'Good, that's stopped them. I wonder if they know as many hymns
as I do. Oo-er, here they come again – another hymn. I will announce
it. *Hymns Ancient and Modern* number 450: "Shall we not love thee,
Mother dear". There's the cock-crow! Why, they're crumbling. The
sun's rising. Saved by the cock. I've beaten them. They can't sing –
the mouths have gone. But they're making a jolly good try. They're
still moving towards me. But they're all dust now. Piles of dust. What's
the good of dust-sheets, at all? I'd better start clearing up. I know,
I'll clean and polish everything since there's still some time before
breakfast. Then I'll put the sheets back and there'll be another
ghostless room in this house for Princess Raskolnikoff!'

'What do you feel was the worst part of the experience?' asked the
princess.
   'Oh, it was all most interesting. Luckily I knew enough hymns to
keep them off until cock-crow . . . Do you know, I like the silk-
handkerchief machine the best. It spins its threads like an insect. It
is steady in its work, like my pulse. Tonight's the last night. I think
I'll spend it in the library.'

'Midnight striking. I need somewhere to sit out the night. I'll get
the sheet off that armchair, just in front of the fire. I wonder if there's

anything under it . . . Ooops! Forgive me, sir. I didn't realise you were smoking your cigar and drinking port under that dust-sheet. What an exceedingly beautiful white beard you wear.'

There was a venerable old man with terrible eyes ensconced under the sheet. Glaring at Sonny, he said, 'Will you just pay my beard out for me while I get up? And hold my glass?' Then he unfolded and unfolded until his head was touching the ceiling.

'Would you like a game of billiards? A drink?' he asked hospitably, still glaring.

'Me, I'm game for anything. Lead on!' said Sonny.

'Sheets away!' said the white-haired creature.

The sheets rose of their own accord off the billiard-table, and off the other items of furniture, and stood about the room like spectators. Sonny was curious. 'What keeps them up? What is really under those sheets, old man?'

'Let me show you,' said the ghoul, catching hold of a sheet and whipping it away. 'You see. Nothing.'

'That nothing which was not there under the sheets almost made me shudder. There are no cues to play with.'

'Abanazar will supply. You will not care to see this, Sonny.'

'Oh, I don't care. Is your name really Abanazar?' Sonny watched unmoved as Abanazar peeled the flesh of his legs and unscrewed the long bones inside to make beautifully smooth ivory cues. It took a metre off the creature's stature. 'I see you are actually a dwarf,' said Sonny.

'Abanazar's the name we can use. Another drink?'

'We need billiard balls.' Abanazar poked his fingers in his head and prised out the two eyeballs. Sonny put the folded beard down on a chair and got his loose change out of his pocket. 'Let's make this more interesting,' he said. 'A penny a hundred?'

'Your soul against mine,' said the diminutive old man.

'Souls. Ah I played cards for my soul the first night; sang for it the second; now I'm playing eye-billiards for it. Leggo. What do you want? Why are you pulling my head?' The dwarf had reached upward and seized Sonny's head in an unbreakable grip.

'We do not have enough balls on the table,' he growled.

Sonny began screaming, then stopped. 'My eyes! Oh my eyes! Oh, that's strange. I can still see. I am on green baize. I am looking up over the cushion of the table at myself carrying a long ivory cue and with a face of hollow bleeding sockets. Yes, I can guide my strokes

15

this way, though I shall soon have black eyes.' Abanazar seemed to use a kind of sonar instead. He stood on a chair to reach the table and uttered a groan before making his stroke.

'Silence, please!' he snapped.

Sonny began clicking his cue against the table-leg to put Abanazar's sonar out. The dwarf missed his stroke, hopped off the chair and began jumping up and down with rage.

'My turn, I think,' said Sonny.

'Give me my cue back,' howled Abanazar.

'I'm sorry. Strict rules of billiards. I must finish my break.'

'You don't understand,' pleaded the dwarf. 'Give me my other leg back. It's your cue.'

'Sorry. Sorry.' Sonny turned his back and went on playing.

'GIVE ME MY LEG.'

'Apart from trying to spoil my game and win my soul, what are you trying to do?'

'I have to go to the loo or I will burst.'

'I see. Without both your legs you can't reach the toilet-bowl.'

'Or I will burst.'

'Sorry. Strict rules.'

'I am bursting!' His eyeless face stretched in all directions and with a prolonged noise like a sea-wave beaching Abanazar burst into briny foam and rubbery shreds of skin. Sonny gleefully snatched his eyes off the table and pushed them back into their sockets.

'His beard exploded too! Luckily most of him went upwards, and hit the ceiling. When can we get married?'

'Now, my darling. Now,' said the princess.

'You see, I have introjected all the ghosts: the magical lunar cats, the hymn-singing agricultural bullies, the dwarfish gigantic magician. Now even less than before have I need to shudder. I just . . . wonder what it's like. Shuddering. But I am too great a hero for that. To shudder . . .'

The wedding was an opulent montage. The grand-duke had returned, and was all over the couple.

'My son! My beloved daughter. How proud the Tsar would have been!' He said this over and over again. His wedding present was the house itself, which he had entirely redecorated. Sonny wanted to know whether their bedroom was one of the previously haunted rooms.

'Ever since your heroic deeds in that house all rooms have been quite clean and quiet,' replied his father-in-law. 'I have had the chapel entirely stripped and refitted as your bridal chamber. Wait until you see the size of the bed. And there is something special about it too, apart from its size. It is time for you both to enter your new home . . .'

'This is where I fought the ghostly congregation with my memory and my voice. There's a light under the door,' said Sonny suspiciously.

'Open it. Carry me across the threshold,' said the bridal princess.

'It's all white! – Like fresh snow.' Sonny was delighted. 'You can hardly see the bed, on that white carpet, with the white walls, in its white hangings and with that white counterpane and white upon white in the great hanging mirrors. It's so white it's quite shivery. With a single red rose on the left-hand pillow – your side, my dear. And hanging above the bed, like a crescent moon, the great ruby-jewelled scimitar of the servitors of the Tsar! This must be what your father meant by special! Never mind, my dear, your bridegroom is fully prepared to match all this magnificence by something special of his own!' Sonny strutted about admiringly.

'What can that be?'

'You'll see. It is a Chinese gift.'

'Chinese!'

'You'll see. Let's get ready for bed. Help me take off the counterpane. Oh ho! It's a great water-bed, look, with fishes swimming like all the ghosts used to through the rooms of this house. But in the brightest colours! Red, blue, gold, look there! Opal! Lapis lazuli! – all kinds of tropical fishes to swim and disport under us as we make love! Ah, Princess, I see it makes you shiver with joy.'

'Is your pulse quite steady still, husband?'

'Oh, yes, it behoves me here to keep calm, just as in the halls of ghosts.' Sonny did up his white pyjamas.

'I am no ghost. Touch me, Sonny. Ah, that's marvellous. Sonny, Sonny . . .'

'Oh Sonny . . . what, haven't you finished yet! Ah, yes, one more time . . .'

'Sonny! Again? You want to do it again?'

He looked down at her fondly. 'I told you I had something to show you which was Chinese.'

'Are you never going to come, and finish and sleep?' She had begun to frown.

'Is it not magnificent? Am I not a hero in bed as well as out of it? No, I never ejaculate. I told you, it's Chinese. Taoist. The monks at the haunted monastery near Ping Pien taught it to me as payment for exorcising their abbot's residence.'

'You mean, you did all that and never felt anything?'

'Of course I did. It felt wonderful.'

'But you've conquered me, Sonny, like you conquered the ghosts. I've given in five times.'

'That's splendid news. As much as you want.'

'That's not the point. I've shuddered by your side and on top of you and under you and the fishes beneath have been in a rainbow whirl while you've been hard and cold like a statue and keeping your pulse quiet and even all the while.'

'Oh that's not fair. Statue? I only just stopped myself shuddering that last time.'

'You total bastard.'

'I . . .'

'You absolute, absolute prick . . .'

'What . . . Princess, what are you going to do with that scimitar.' She had stood up on the wobbly bed and snatched the great half-moon blade from the wall. She waved it over him, and the reverberation of the water-bed made this extremely hazardous.

'How do you know I won't cut your thing off to make sure you shudder in your death-throes?'

'Princess . . . be reasonable.'

'No talk now, Sonny. I am not conversable. I am not a ghost. This is the end for you!'

Sonny screamed as she brought the blade down, split the water-bed open and collapsed laughing in its watery rains. Sonny lay there, his eyes covered, shuddering in long slow convulsions. He thought he was weltering in his own blood. Then he sat up and looked around him. 'Oh, I'm shuddering all over. Wonderful! Look at the fishes, tickling us like a multitude of ghosts! What a surprise! What a coming! Look how I shudder. Everything's wet. I feel wonderful, like a real hero at last. Thank you, Princess, oh thank you . . .'

But the Princess was busy rescuing the fishes. The soaked frills of her elaborate white nightdress looked like the gills of some mermaid, half-human, half-watercreature. Sonny could not take his eyes off her as she scrambled about among the hopping fish, and he shuddered with happiness.

A Job at Holle Park

A Job at Holle Park

Kate hurried after the famous female inventor and entrepreneur as she bulldozed her way at a great pace through the terraces and marvels of Holle Park shouting instruction and encouragement as she went.

Three years ago, from the waste-pits and water-slums of the Surrey gravel-works, a magnificent theme park had arisen.

Kate blinked in wonder as they passed the vast and numerous pavilions shining in the pale March sunlight, each entrance temptingly ajar, waiting for the fun to start.

She was here! She was here! At Holle Park!

Yesterday, after an unholy row with her mother and her ugly spoilt-brat kid sister, she'd walked out with only what she had on her back and in her pockets and hitched down south.

Kate looked at the army of men and women moving purposefully from area to area preparing for the Easter opening. She longed to be one of them!

She jumped back smartly as a Victorian omnibus clattered by, drawn by two massive shire-horses. The smell of horse-sweat and leather dazed her, the driver cracked his whip high in the air. 'Get-along, get-along,' he yelled, and as she gawped she stumbled back into the arms of a human-sized Mickey Mouse. Apologising, she sprinted up the slope and around the side of the Chaplin Pavilion. Far ahead Miss Holle had already turned the corner of the Stone

Tent of Miracles and was disappearing into the Elgar Subway. Kate ran after her, through the subway and past the Thomas Hardy Greenhouse, into and out of the Marie Stopes Gift Shop and Coffee House, and along the north edge of the James Joyce Centre for Lost Children.

It's true that they do nothing by halves here, thought Kate, panting, thanking her lucky stars for her meeting with Miss Holle first thing this morning. Kate had been leaning over the Wishing Well of Wonderful Wisdom (just outside the main gates), sobbing her heart out, when the tall shadow of Miss Roberta Holle had blotted out the sun. 'What's wrong?' she'd asked. Kate had sobbed, and sniffed, 'I need a j . . . j . . . job, Ma'am. Please. I've read everything I can about your great park.'

Now Kate was catching her up. They raced past the pub, the Chariot of Parrots, and down a gentle incline into the funfair.

Here was every ride ever dreamed of. Want to spin round dizzily in a huge Crown Derby teacup seating eight? Want to fly to the stars inside a transparent centaur? Want to whiz round fastened by cunning straps into a great spider's web? Need to helterskelter down inside a coiling wriggly snake? Fancy shooting down a giant glass tube, all the kids like elements in a great chemical adventure-experiment? Like to ride on a witch's broom through starry skies? How about scooting down the Devil's Drop? There were baby rides for little 'uns on the backs of kindly animaux. There was the great black carcass of a submarine for simulating great moments from the Second World War. And there were many more rides: the Locust Run, the Water Basket, the Pig in a Wheelbarrow, the Tantrum Teaser, the Chinese Bounce-Pagoda, the famous Ozymandias Stretch-Bump, the Dreaming Slope, the Sliding Heart.

Mark, a boy from the Kangaroo Rides, brought Kate a Tower Burger and a Coke. They sat in the Fiscal Gardens, among the six-foot topiary dollars, pounds, yen, francs and marks, admiring the flower-beds planted out to depict bank-notes and coins. In their Holle Park uniforms they made a fine couple; Kate in black and scarlet embroidered with little silver skulls, Mark in blue, with a gold kangaroo-motif on his sweatshirt.

The park was already showing a profit after only six weeks. Every day, two hours or so after the gates opened, they were shut again, as capacity was reached. The vast size of the park, however, prevented any sordid crowding. Roberta Holle had insisted at all planning meetings on the importance of the visitor's sense of space and vista. 'Individuals not hordes' was her motto.

'Wouldn't have your job, love,' Mark said.

'Why not?' Kate asked. 'It's only a kind of ghost train.'

'Yuck, yuck.'

Aiming her straw, Kate blew the last of her Coke in his face.

'My favourite ghoul,' she teased, fending him off with smacks, 'is the Random-Ransacker, the man who specialises in . . .'

'Don't tell me, don't tell me . . .'

'How about the Ghoul Queen then, who bites off girls' breasts? . . . or . . .'

'God, it would give me terrible dreams.'

'Not me. I have lovely dreams.'

They kissed.

The next huddle of punters stooped down the entrance tunnel of the Gothic Ghoul Grotto and threaded their way squealing ('It's dark, it's dark – I don't *like* this, DAD!') through a maze where they were serenaded by answering groans and gales of bedlam laughter and the banshee arias of a dozen lost souls; they stampeded past the orchestra of jazz-ghouls and underneath the archway of gibbets, dodging the dangling feet of the dead men and then up a narrow scary ladder ('MUM, GET ME OUT OF HERE!' 'It's all right, Johnny, there's n – n – nothing to be – AARGH!!!') through which skeletal fingers pinched and poked and then in a final spurt they all dashed along a metallic floored alleyway and down to an arena where assistants dressed as Ghoul Girls (Kate was one, a probationary ghoul) helped them (two by two) into swaying mini-hearse-like conveyances that ran on a trackway. Off went the riders, on their journey of scenic horrors; past the horrible Doctor Cypher with his demon nurses, slowly rotating and flinching in their black chairs until they confronted the Snarling Pig-Woman of Padstow, round again and up the slope (hot smells of fear and sweat) to show the shocking sight of the winged-man monster Lupus-Mundus drooling over his victims tied up in string like so many parcels, on to the Giant Black Hen of Hounslow, then to the Ghoul Queen herself, with her throttling hands and her taste for raw breasts; even those who wanted to close their eyes now could not, they watched every horror with dry mouths and gulping breath, but the ride went on, the carts turned with their moaning occupants, and next came the

Birmingham Baby-Killer, then the fiery-eyed and retributive Dracula (an old friend much enjoyed especially by the younger visitors who greeted him with shouts of 'Nice to see you back, Drac'); but then they quivered as they passed within a hair's breadth of the Windlesham Owl-Beast, and even the men felt pretty sick when the Death-Waltzers tiptoed into sight; the air was close, it was very dark, the electric candles flickered and dimmed then flared up when least expected to reveal the Four Children of the Apocalypse (the shrieks of the visitors mingled with the soundtrack shrieks of the tableaux, the thunck of the axe of the Boy Clown, the terrible croak of the Gorgon, the great and awful whispering of the Serpent of the Fire); then the carts were drawn past the Long House of the Summer Ghosts, to the final shock – their own faces pulled like toffee in the banks of distorting mirrors that led to the exit.

On her first day, Kate overheard a small child pipe up, 'Can we go round again, Mum?' Trotting after his parents, he persisted. 'Mum, can we, can we?' An imperious maternal 'no' echoed down the tunnel. Kate's heart swelled with pride, gladdened.

Every evening Kate was the one who volunteered to stay late to oil the automata, and check the mechanics of the ghoul-track and ghoul-carts. She liked the grotto. It was mysteriously comforting to her – she found in there an intensity of purpose which her life had lacked before; she was thankful to the ghouls in ways she didn't yet understand for making her own fears and fantasies bearable. Only now after the first month working here did she realise how she had feared the blood of her own body, and how the fantasy of killing a child had often excited and depressed her; now, as she moved in the shadows of the grotto, her own shadowed self moved into the light, was happier, freer, ready for life.

She wasn't afraid of getting her hands dirty. Her hands were grimed-in with the black, nothing got it out completely. Sometimes she burned her hands on the over-heated metal but she loved her job and took great pride in servicing the machinery and making all safe.

She rented a room in the nearby town and relished her independence. The ghouls with their stiff dances and serious thoughts were her friends. She looked on them as the forms of human instinct, seen so exaggeratedly that everyone's own cruelty was drawn out and gentled by them.

Roberta Holle called her into the office. She looked calculatingly at Kate.

'Another ten quid a week. And the position of Chief Ghoul Girl. How does it sound to you, Kate?'

Kate looked at her boss in amazement.

'Thank you, Miss Holle.' She ran round and kissed Roberta lightly on the cheek.

Blushing, the older woman said casually, 'How's that young man of yours then?'

The glass-canopied green-hulled pleasure boat glided over the pearl-grey water. On her day off Kate often went over the water to the park farm. The animals, the young squirmy piglets, the fluffy lambs, the wobbly calves, made a change after the ghouls. She leaned over the side and looked down at the clear water. Despite her happiness at Holle Park, she was sometimes homesick, even for her nagging mother and her sulky strut-about sister, Alice.

All summer the sun shone down on Holle Park. It shone on the roof of the Amphora Spa and on the roof of the Lilliput Circus. It shone on the roof of the Peacock Cloister (mosaics and quiet seats for the elderly). It shone on the enormous Nappy-Pin that crowned the Baby-Changing Rotunda and glanced off the drawn blinds of the Golden-Lap Casino (open nights only); it shone on the khaki curtains of the Kitbag and Kettle Canteen; it glinted fierily off the roof of the Pleasure of Mirrors (no distorting mirrors in here but cleverly enhancing ones, putting everyone in a good mood, everyone was beautiful). It shone on the dark roof of the Planetarium; it shone down on the River of Dreams, a slow and meandering boat-ride through scented gardens with sweet light-classical music playing. Yes, Holle Park was a world in itself, better than the world, reflecting it and improving it, intent only on pleasure. On the flagpole at the great gates, the national flag snapped and cracked, patriotic colours nailed tight to the blue sky. And beyond, the many pagodas and pylons, spires and domes of the park flowered, profound and curious city.

From their penthouse office high in the Saint Judith Persiflage Building (named for their dear mother, in her Swiss convent) Roberta and Georgina Holle linked arms and smiled down on their creation.

Whereas Roberta was the inventor, designer, dreamer and mother of Holle Park, Georgina, the beauty of the two sisters, was the financial genius and father. The cyphers and lamentations of money were music in her ears. On paper, on computer, money sprang to her call, her song; money came to her, land, buildings, lakes, ships, machines, goods; antiques, commodities of all kinds came to her, in their endless transformations. Even estimates for the perimeter fencing, for the uniforms of the security men, delighted Georgina, were individual phrases in the great symphony she composed with money. Like her elder sister, she was a large woman; but where Roberta dressed as a cowboy, in high boots, jeans and checked shirt, Georgina was sweetly, softly, sensuously feminine. Dressed in pastel shades, she was all long flowering skirts and embroidered blouses, gold chains, bracelets, brooches, lockets, be-ringed hands with long fingernails pinkly-enamelled; nevertheless her seductive unchallenging voice ruled the boardroom, her implacable placidity and platinum-blonde powers dazzling male colleagues and female rivals, and she drove her staff before her in an ecstasy of obedience to her will.

Oliver, her secretary, coming to her summons, smiled flirtatiously at her, sat down, crossed his legs, flipped open his dictation book, looked up, expectant, adoring, at his beloved boss. Smiling kindly at Oliver, Georgina dictated through delicately glossed lips, in her pure and serene tones: 'Dear Mr Fanfaron, I cannot accept your Board's recent statement that our two companies cannot merge. Allow me to point out that Holle Enterprises Universal, in the form of our subsidiary Fallen Angels Ltd, now own 40 per cent of voting stock in your Fetish Fun Plc, and that a recent survey of your stockholders leads us to believe that they look favourably upon the proposed merger . . .'

Very early every morning, several hours before the park opened, Kate unlocked the back entrance of the grotto and went into the little storeroom. Her routine was to inspect and re-grime the exhibits every day, tinkering and adding odd touches wherever necessary. She conscientiously kept up the cankered mildewed look for which the grotto was famous.

Hefting the stepladder on her shoulder and picking up her box of tricks, she began her rounds. She puffed some theatrical dust on to a clean cloth and delicately applied the new dirt to the spun-glass faces of the ghouls. She sprayed them tenderly with cobweb. To her they all had beauty and purpose, even the Blood-Dribbling Dwarf and the Spanking Postman. Climbing her ladder, she rearranged the demon rats and satirical spiders that peered down from the balcony of the Bedlam Hotel and sprinkled handfuls of strange feculence generously about, a daub of guano here, a shower of plastic fleas there, a smutch of scuff here, a slubber of offal there, a filth of fur over there. All these ministrations improved the ravaged rottenness of the grotto, a housekeeping in reverse.

Next, she made herself busy replacing the various cartridges of artificial blood and ghoul-spit, unblocking any stoppages with a pipe-cleaner. She re-yellowed several sets of bared teeth, and renewed much snot and phlegm. She repainted the tears of blood the Ghoul Queen shed and the green gunge many of the ghouls oozed. Taking a damp oily rag, she rubbed it over the twisted festering faces of the Bad Babies in the Hell Nursery, admiring, as she worked, the fly-blown and rotting-pear texture of their hideous features.

She had a worried moment when she thought she'd run out of artificial vomit but luckily there was one sachet left which she tore open and squelched over the carpet of the Castle of Amputations. Hands on hips, she looked around with pride and said, 'Now, what next . . . ?'

Last night Roberta Holle had given her a special air-freshener just perfected in her laboratory. It was in fact an air-sourer and as Kate pressed the button gusts of mortuary air choked her. 'That's great,' she coughed. She remembered Miss Holle's instructions. 'I'm trusting you, Kate, to ensure my ghouls always look their very worst, as uncongenial and beastly as possible. I want nastiness levels kept high at all times, and you must make sure that this Charnel Number Five keeps the atmosphere nicely polluted, OK?'

Kate sighed happily. The diabolic inhabitants of the grotto were all set for the day's visitors. How hideous and warped they all looked. Kate grinned affectionately. She heard Mark whistling outside. He wouldn't come in here.

'I'll be done soon,' she called to him.

'We'll have breakfast,' he said, peering cautiously through the door.

Bank Holiday. Spring Bank Holiday. Damn. Damn. Why on a Bank Holiday? By midday Kate knew something was wrong. She sensed it. She had a word with the girls, telling them to keep a look-out, then got in one of the cars, ignoring the screams around her, and scrutinised all the exhibits, one by one. It was even hotter than usual in the grotto

and the graveyard stink was like a huge invisible cloud everywhere.
Kate's head ached. She was upset. She didn't like things to go wrong.
She was responsible! The Windlesham Owl-Beast was OK, his red
eyes flashing nicely. Doctor Cypher and his mad nurses were gibbering
beautifully, Dracula, the old dependable, was biting his victim with
customary verve, the four hideous Children of the Apocalypse were
sucking bones as intently as ever. Oh no! It was The Ghoul Queen
herself, with her necklace of severed heads; her greedy hands should
have been stretched out, fingers flexed for throats to tear, her scaly
skin should have been rippling and seething with guck, her mouth
should have been opening and closing in a convulsive snarl, but she
was just standing like a lazy schoolgirl, head down. 'Tut, tut,' murmured Kate, relieved to find the culprit, hoping that the punters were
too scared to notice, praying that no regulars would complain, that
Miss Holle wouldn't do one of her random inspections.

'I'll see to you later,' she said to the Ghoul Queen.

The park closed at ten o'clock. Kate had a quick sandwich and a beer,
and went back to the grotto. Taking her toolbox from the storeroom,
she clambered into the Ghoul Queen's chamber. The grotto was
arranged on three spiral levels, to use all the available space, and to
disorient the visitor. The exhibits were in a kind of stack, with the
trackway winding anti-clockwise up and round. Above Kate was
Doctor Cypher; below, the Pig-Woman of Padstow. All was quiet.
She unvelcroed the Ghoul Queen's bikini top and unscrewed the
panel in her back. Shining her torch in, she checked the wiring
and the circuits. Everything seemed normal. Nothing wrong. Now
why . . . ? She pondered. It was still hot and stuffy in there, smelly
with the day's aftermath, odours of fear and fright and sweat and
decay-aerosol. Kate wiped a greasy handkerchief over her face. Must
be a loose connection somewhere. Look again. She peered into the
Ghoul Queen's face; the eyeballs seemed fine, the mouth (she stuck
her fingers right in and felt around) was OK, teeth sharp and all
securely in place; she waggled the arms and hands; nothing rattled.
She poked the ears and tapped the skull. No. Nothing wrong. The
Ghoul Queen sneered back. Kate was tired; it had been a long
day. 'Come on, old girl,' she groaned. Stepping back, she frowned.
Suddenly she gave the robot an experimental biff in the belly (the
technician's familiar second line of approach) and was rewarded by a
metallic groan and the slow-lunge forward of the killing arms. Kate

dodged, nodding. 'Good, good, good,' she said. 'Gotcha!' she said, gazing fondly in the Ghoul Queen's yellow eyes. The android suddenly shrieked. 'Fine,' said Kate, kneeling down and rapping at the Ghoul Queen's ankles, which had given trouble before. They checked out. She reached across to the control box hidden under a pile of plastic skeletons and switched the power off; the Ghoul Queen froze in mid-howl. Kate screwed her back-panel into place, straightened the bikini top, turned the power on again and then off for the night. She patted the Ghoul Queen on the shoulder. All was well. Kate left the grotto, yawning. The robots, if they could love at all, loved Kate with a grisly cadaverous love.

Kate smiled whitely. Her mother and sister were all over her. Their greedy love, their insincerity, the ill-concealed self-interest of the pair were the most ghoulish things Kate had ever known. And I suppose, she thought with surprise, I'm an expert.

Miss Roberta had given her three days' leave; tears of homesickness had shocked Kate and Roberta Holle as she made her daily report to the boss.

Her mother kissed her yet again. 'My dear, dear Kate,' she said, her smile all negotiation and expectation.

'Hi, Mum. Hello, Alice.'

'Sister Kate, sit here, this is the nicest chair. Get down, Butch.'

Alice scruffed the old cat outside.

'Sit here, Kate dear. Have this cake. I am so proud of you, my clever girl. Imagine. Miss Roberta Holle *herself.*'

Kate's mother sat across the table from her, smiling and smiling, nodding, her hands fidgeting greedily.

'Alice,' she said sharply, 'more hot water for Kate's tea, and more of my best fruit cake.'

'I'm fine, Mum.'

'Nonsense, that sister of yours has got to wake her ideas up. Get off her bum for a change. Here, dear Kate.'

She handed Kate another cup of tea. It was the best china, too.

'Tell me more about your job, dear, and about the famous Holle sisters.' Kate's mother leaned forward, her eyes feasting on her fortunate daughter. 'Bonuses, you said?'

'Tell us,' wheedled Alice, her long thin spotty face pressed close to her sister's.

'I have to work pretty hard, you know,' pointed out Kate.

'Sounds a breeze to me,' said Alice under her breath.

'Share and share alike, eh?' Kate's ma tickled her own itchy palm meaningfully. Kate said nothing.

'What are you doing here?' Kate stared at her sister in amazement.

'I'm on the payroll now.'

'I suppose you're one of the temporaries I asked for. But can you do it?'

''Course I can. Gonna get my uniform.' Alice pranced away.

'What's the problem, Sandra?'

Kate leaned over the back stair balcony. Her deputy looked up irritably. Before she could speak Alice whined, 'She wants me to oil these horrid things. Ugh, I'll get dirty. She's a bully, Kate.'

'Alice!'

'And I hate those . . . things. They're spooky. I won't do it.'

'Alice!'

'Ma said you were to look after me.'

The summer was a scorcher. She walked by one of the four swimming pools, the Proserpine Pool, with its mosaic floor depicting the marriage of Proserpine and Pluto, and there was her sister Alice sunbathing by the poolside in her bikini bottoms, surrounded by admiring young men. She'd shed her uniform of black T-shirt and leggings patterned with tiny silvery winged skulls, and her black-lace beret, tossing them aside on the grass.

Kate took a deep breath, straightened her armband, which read SUPERVISOR, and smacked Alice hard on the leg.

'Hey!' Alice and the boys looked lazily at her.

'Alice, get back on duty.'

'Yuck! It's too dark and slimy in there. You go. I'm' – she yawned – 'OK here.'

Kate glared. 'Alice, you're here to work.'

'Oh pooh! Don't be boring. Isn't she boring?' The young men sniggered aggressively.

Kate stalked away.

Late in August the drought broke. Torrential rain fell all night. The storm dropped abruptly at dawn, the thunder rolled away. But by then the damage had been done. Much of the park was flooded. The fire brigade arrived in dependable kindergarten colours, to pump and to salvage what they could.

Kate, Sandra, and Jack from Maintenance stood with water lapping at their knees. The ghoul-grotto was awash. Kate was almost in tears as Jack swung the torch around. The ghouls stared hopelessly at them. Shreds of gut and gore, a torn petticoat from the Pig-Woman, and other ghoulish debris, corpse-toys from the Children of the Apocalypse, a few skeletal fingers, swirled around them.

'I reckon we'll lose a good many of 'em,' said Kate. 'They'll rust, you see.'

Sandra nodded, sniffing.

'Poor Miss Roberta,' Kate added.

Miss Roberta had been summoned home immediately from Rome, where she was researching her latest project, the Vatican Horror (due to open in two years' time).

'We'd better make a start. Let's move them all out, dismantle 'em, dry 'em, hair-dryers we'll need, and then renovate what we can.'

'OK, Kate.'

The three of them had already carried out the Bad Babies, the Blood-Dribbling Dwarf, the Pig-Woman, the Ghoul Queen and the Spanking Postman and laid them gently on polythene sheeting in the pick-up truck before Alice turned up, scowling and complaining about having to come in on her day off.

'This is an emergency,' Kate snapped. 'You look sharp and bring out Dracula.'

With a sneering sigh, Alice sploshed reluctantly inside, not even answering Jack's greeting as he staggered out with the Windlesham Owl-Beast dripping in his arms. He lowered it into the truck, goggling his eyes at Kate. She grinned back at him. 'You know,' she said, 'I think most of these can be saved! Look, the basic trouble is going to be – '

A loud thud, a splash and a shriek interrupted her. Another shriek, and another rang out. Kate looked questioningly at Jack and then ran inside. Alice was struggling in three feet of water with Dracula, his coat-tails flying and his mouth spewing fake blood all over the stupid girl, who howled in panic. 'Kate, do something!' But Kate burst out laughing. Alice's comic anger broke the tension of the morning. She screamed with frustration, splashing and spluttering, until Jack and Sandra freed her from Dracula and lugged him away. Alice beat frantically at the robot until it was out of her reach.

'Alice, are you all right?' Kate giggled.

'Stop laughing at me!' Alice batted the water with both hands, soaking Kate from head to foot.

'Stupid. What do you expect? You didn't hold Dracula like I showed you. You never pay attention, Alice. You're so lazy and lub-handed.'

Alice lurched forward and shoved her sister hard.

'Know-all. I hate you! Freak-lover!'

'You're fired. Get your week's wages at the office.'

'I was quitting anyway. You wait till I tell Ma.'

Alice squelched out, tears of spite streaking her filthy face.

'Sorry about your sister, Kate.'

'She's happier at home, Miss Roberta.'

The two women were carefully inspecting the refurbished robots, set out in a row in the courtyard outside Miss Holle's workshop. In the sunlight their varied gruesomenesses looked gay and jaunty. The ghouls smelt lovely, of new paint and fresh oil. 'But we'll soon fix that,' said Miss Holle. She and Kate and Jack and young Mr Holyhead from the museum had worked flat out for six weeks.

'Ghoul-worthy,' said Roberta cheerfully, 'though I speak as shouldn't.'

'Open for business?'

'You bet, Kate.'

The house smelt of cats and the sourness of flowers left rotting in unchanged water.

Cross as crabs, Alice and her mother sat in the kitchen. The sink was piled with dirty dishes. The floor was dirty, unswept. A litter of newspapers covered the table. Two old cats snoozed on a grubby sofa. The room was dimly lit from a single unshaded bulb. Outside the rain fell frumpishly.

With a groan, the elder woman got to her feet and shuffled over to the window.

'Oh Alice, why have you let the garden go? Look at it, just a wilderness now. Kate always kept it so nice, geraniums, mimulus, fuchsias, begonias, daffs in the spring.'

'Shut up, Ma.'

'Look at this kitchen. Nothing gets done any more. Them stairs haven't been vacuumed in six months. The beds haven't been changed in God knows how long. One of these bloody cats has been sick in the hall. You cleared it up yet? No, not you, madam.'

'Stop whining, you old cow.'

'I can't do the work any more, girl.'

'Old, old, old *bag*.' Alice glared at her mother.

The old woman shivered. 'It's cold in here.'

'Hey Ma, I want some money.'

'Money! You had fifty quid from Kate yesterday, same as me. Where's it gone?'

Alice glared. 'None of your business.' The girl leaned over and grabbed her mother's purse. 'Gimme.'

'I'll tell Kate. I'll ring her. Or I'll write.'

Alice laughed nastily.

'I don't care.' She slummocked upstairs to get herself dolled up.

'Out every bleeding night,' her mother muttered angrily. Picking up one of the old newspapers, she re-read the front-page news. It had been in all the tabloids, even a feature on page five of *The Times* (posh Mrs Moody in the chemist told her that), the first marriage to be solemnised at Holle Park in the brand-new One Flesh Wedding Bower. She stared at her daughter Kate's happy smile and at Mark's good looks under the banner headline, GHOUL GIRL GETS HER MARK. A curious expression of sulky pride flickered over the old woman's face. For the thousandth time she read: 'Kate and Mark are to honeymoon in Spain, in a private villa owned by Miss Roberta Holle, the famous Cortina d'Oro; and on their return to this country will take up senior appointments in the Holle organisation . . .'

'Ma!'

Alice ripped the paper from her hand and, bundling them up, chucked the tattered newspapers out into the coalhole.

'Kate's finished with us, Ma. The money each week and that's our lot. That's the deal.'

'Alice!'

'I said, she's finished with us!'

Kate put her mother's letter unopened with all the others at the back of the drawer. There's monsters and monsters, she thought. From the big picture window of their apartment (given to them freehold as a wedding gift from the Holle sisters) she looked down at the shining blue lakes and the many glittering white buildings (her own beloved grotto small-crouching among them) of Holle Park; with a shiver of love knew that this was home. She turned and smiled at Mark.

The Flounder

The flounder

The wife was complaining about the stink again. Personally, I couldn't smell it. When the farmer had let us have the old barn I thought I might do it up a bit. But when I had swept the old straw out, and put new straw in the big manger with a bit of a tarpaulin over it for our bed, it looked so cosy I didn't want to change anything. So I nailed a bit of lino over the roof where the rain came in, and that was it. It all looked and smelt very cosy to me.

But she would keep on. Times were bad. I took her to the door and showed her the offshore factory ships lit up like a city or a carnival or solid fireworks. 'How grand and beautiful they look,' she said, 'they hover on the horizon like castles in the air.' Indeed they did, but they were still overfishing the area. That was why we were poor.

'At least go out and catch something to eat,' she said. Well, I like a quiet life, and a smoke in the open air, so I trudged down the beach to where I had set my line. The water was so clear and peaceful I could see it trailing off almost to the shingle bottom. I didn't think I dared go back until I had caught something. But there were no fish, thanks to those ships. But – steady – there was a struggle in the water. Something had bitten. A big 'un. I hauled it in, not without difficulty. I like to talk aloud when I am by myself.

'A flounder! It's an enormous flounder!' I said to nobody in particular.

'No, I'm not,' it said. I often heard voices in the wind and the waves, but this had an *external* quality. I thought it came from the fish. Nobody could blame me for replying.

'If you're not a flounder, what are you then?' I looked in my basket for the gaff.

'I'm an enchanted prince.' There was a Spanish lisp to the cultivated tones. It was the hook, I guessed.

'Of course you are.' I must have left the gaff at home. I would have to stun my prize with a stone. 'But my wife and I are very hungry. If you're a prince, it's the likes of you that take the food from our mouths, so here's your opportunity to put it back again. But I think you're a flounder, and a flounder is simple food.'

'If I'm a prince, are you a cannibal? Alternatively, would a talking flounder taste right?'

I sat down on a stone and scratched my head.

'You've got something there,' I said. 'I'd better let you go.'

'Thank you. I'm obliged,' said the flounder, as I unhooked him.

So there went our dinner, diving to the bottom, leaving a long streak of blood behind it in the water. I now had the task of explaining.

My wife had the pan hot, but she grasped the situation as soon as I told her.

'You idiot! Do you mean to tell me you let it go without wishing for anything?'

'Wishing? No, I didn't think of wishing.' I never did, really. I am a fairly contented sort of person.

'My husband tells me that he let an enchanted fish go because he couldn't think of anything to wish, while here I am slaving my life away in a *hovel* that stinks and is hopping with fleas, a *hovel*, with our married bed a cattle-manger full of straw! Go back at once. Tell it we want a cottage. A neat little cottage with a herb garden and a scallop-shell path. That's the least it could do.'

I didn't want to go back. The weather was thickening up. So was the storm at home. I half-heard her explaining that such a fish could let us off the hook of our poverty. It might have been hissing in her skillet by now, so it must be grateful. I wasn't even sure that it was real. But I loved her, and would pretend for her sake.

The sea by the time I got to it again looked like a malicious machine, turning on green hinges. I packed up my tackle, all the while thinking of the little ceremonious poem I would make up as bait for magic, if magic there were. That was it! A bit rough, but just a bit of a *speil* or spell.

> 'Platichthys princeps, *princely fish,*
> *Come from your depths and grant my wish*
> *For this is the day I saved your life;*
> *Fair's fair, I must please my wife;*
> *Slide your head through the water's noose,*
> *Fear not – I am the one who set you loose.'*

The big head with its goggling gold eyes came up through the jalousies of the water.

'I know what she wants.'

'A little cottage . . .'

'She's got it.' That was that. Instant magic.

I trudged up the beach again and looked for our barn. It was nowhere to be seen. The shingle slopes were uneven, and the weather confusing. Obviously I had come out at a different place. I noticed a prim little stuccoed cottage with lace curtains and rather a good-looking young-middle-aged woman in a white apron walking down the path. I was surprised when she spoke brightly to me over the gate.

'There you are then!'

'Beg pardon?'

'I was right, you see. Not that we can afford to retire, and we'll need a bit more cash to keep this place going, but we'll make a handsome picture at the end of the day sitting in front of our fine cottage, me with my fresh apron and you with your pipe as the sun goes down over the sea, source of our living and home of our benefactor.' I came to earth suddenly; it was my wife staring anxiously into my face and waiting for me to say something. I saw she was very happy. I was naturally pleased, but also knew that I was worried. Wasn't magic supposed to be habit-forming? I took out my pipe.

'You'll keep that awful tobacco right out of my house!' I put it away again. She wanted to show me round.

You could see by the exposed coigns that the stucco was laid over good granite blocks: the rock of ages. The flounder had not cheated us over materials. There was a narrow hall and the first room was the front parlour. I doubted whether that would ever be used, except for a funeral. Hers or mine. I peered round the door and got an impression of chintz and pot-pourri.

The back room was more interesting. It was a kitchen–diner, and very well lit, with windows at the east and south. Fitted cupboards made the kitchen area very smart; there were broad counters and an electric cooker with a rotisserie. There was a refrigerator, of course, but I noticed she had put the milk bottles on the slate shelf of the pantry, which was set in the thickness of the cool stone. I opened the kitchen door and went out into the herb garden, which smelt of twilight and itself. The full moon was just beginning to rise. I opened the door of one of the lean-tos built against the back garden wall; it was a nice clean whitewashed but earth-smelling little crapper. The other shed would hold garden tools, but I wasn't so. interested in these. My wife's hand stole into mine. I put my arm round her waist. The moon slid higher.

I woke in the big brass bedstead, which nearly filled our upstairs bedroom, to the sound of crashing saucepans and shrill curses. I hastily pulled on a pair of trousers and went downstairs. I could feel my wife's rage as soon as I opened the little cupboard doorway into the living-room. It was like a wall of heat.

'Oh, there you are. You'd better get to work. I've got a job for you. I can't bloody well cook a meal with you hanging around. Kill me a chicken. Here's the hatchet.' She nearly took my nose off as she thrust it at me. 'I'm all elbows in this cramped little hole. Why didn't that damn fish give us a bigger place? Just by looking at you he could tell we'd want to keep out of each other's way most of the time. So, my *dear* husband, when you've slaughtered that bird, go to that flounder of yours and say we want something bigger. Much bigger. A castle will do. And everything that goes with it . . .'

As she spoke I became aware that the weather was playing up. The light went greyer, and the wind began to whine on the edge of the house. I found it difficult to hear all she was saying, because changes in weather get me like that, but it didn't matter – the message was clear.

'A castle, yes that would do nicely . . . a castle with lands . . . and with the lands, a title . . . ah, very nice, honour and earth, earth and honour . . . and a titled castle, a castled title . . .'

The next thing I knew I was on the beach again and doing my recitation to a sea you couldn't see through, a sea that looked like phlegm, with black rafts of seaweed scudding past, small heavy waves falling like the headman's axe, and surf that hissed like acid.

The Flounder

'Platichthys princeps, *princely fish,*
Rise through your depths and grant my wish,
Slip your head through your salty sky,
Grant me my wish, and don't ask why,
Just yesterday I saved your life,
Fair's fair, I must please my wife.'

A faint mist had formed on the troubled water, and through it I heard the cultivated tones.

'I know what she wants.'

'A castle.'

'She's got it.'

I waited for more. The mist faded and there was nobody there. So I turned away from the slimy evil-looking sea and took the shingled beach at a run. I wanted to see our castle.

I got up to the top, and there was nothing there but a road and a bus-stop. I crossed the road and saw a bus coming in the distance. I put up my hand and it stopped. The panel at the front said COURTESY BUS – TO THE CASTLE. That was just as well. I had no money. There were some lead weights in my pocket, but I doubt if they would have bought me a ride.

The castle was magnificent! My legs felt quite weak as I got down the bus steps. I am sure my mouth was hanging open. On the face of it, it was a sprawling late-medieval manor house, but some genius had given it a nervous baroque energy. As I stumbled towards it, the apparent rectitude of the perpendicular tracery of the many windows resolved itself into a multitude of serpentine forms, vigorous, tense and unstable, with a profusion of restless detail. It was like walking into a magnified bundle of hair, or a wig, never quite still. It made you want to run, or dance, but not to sing. The porch resembled the baldacchino by Bernini, the great bronze canopy over the high altar in St Peter's, darkly magnificent, the barley-sugar columns twisting like black flames, like a diabolic reflection of some rite to be performed beneath, on the broad front step, over which I tiptoed like a phantom.

The cathedral-like doors of brass and ebony were wide open. Inside was a half-timbered hall with a stone floor and a hammerbeam roof. Leaning against a rack of pikes was a man dressed in green and black doublet and hose, a ruff, and an elaborate hair-do, which seemed to be gilded. He was cleaning his nails with a slender dagger. I coughed discreetly.

'Hello?' The tall fellow went on cleaning his nails. His doublet and hose were slashed over white silk underthings, so, when he shifted his position to face away from me, the colours of his clothes shifting over each other reminded me of the evil-looking sea where I had wished these monstrous accommodations into being. I moved until we were facing again and put out my hand to tap him on the breast. The poignard ceased its action. Two fingers passed down its blade, removing traces of some tarry substance. In a very relaxed fashion, it was pointing at me. The green eyes under the shining hair looked at me coolly.

'Save you,' drawled this Osric.

'And you, sir.' The other shrugged, dropped his eyes, and resumed taking his nails out of mourning.

'I'm sorry to bother you.' Another shrug. 'Can you direct me to my wife?'

'What wife?' He appeared slightly stimulated.

'The Lady of the Manor.' His eyebrows shot up into his gilt hairline. 'My Lady will descend into the great hall in three minutes precisely.' Then he looked at me again, and smiled unexpectedly.

'You have no weapon,' he said, taking the dagger-blade in his left hand and my hand in his right, and laying the hilt in my palm and closing my fingers over it.

'Without rank, nobody needs a weapon,' he hissed, 'but if you are who you say you are . . .', and he was gone like a walking portion of the flounder's domain. And fishy enough.

I sat down for a moment to rest my legs and to ruminate about the politics of a set-up like this. I was startled by a blazing light and clatter coming down the corridor. It was a brazier on an iron trolley, full of red coals. Two men were lighting torches at it and slipping them into wall-brackets. One of them spoke to me.

'You can't sit here. Who are you?'

'Well, I'm . . . her husband, that's who I am.'

'Whose husband?'

'You could say . . . I'm the man of the house.'

'Yer what?'

'I'm the Lord of the Manor.'

'Lord . . .' They both started laughing. But then my friend in green and black appeared again, and gave them a look. They hurriedly resumed hanging up their torches, while from the recesses of the high stone corridor a glittering procession made its way towards me.

44

My wife led the company. She looked – well – imposing. She wore a black velvet gown barred all in gold and with immense sleeves lined with white fur. In it she resembled the world's vagina. The people who fluttered around her had perhaps been chosen so that they were all smaller than she was, and this of course added to the effect of Queen Termite of the Hive. I had on my fisherman's gear, the same as I went down to the beach in, but I am a good six foot, a head taller than she is. So when I stood up I was noticed. I think otherwise she would simply have swept past, and I would have had to make my way with the servants. She crooked her finger at me, and did a sort of shimmy inside her gown, so that panels of sequins sewn on it made her look as though she were standing in a dark and glittering fire.

'There you are,' she said to me, but sideways to her companions as well. 'This is a little better, isn't it? You'll have plenty to do around this place. Have you seen the big pigsties in the orchard? Pork and apple, you know. I'll put you in charge of them. Damme, it's good to have servants but there are so many mouths to feed. I want you to manage the estate so it becomes self-sufficient. Or you can be my jester. Take your pick. Let me have music there, ho!' A kind of droning music filled the air, from a species of lyre with a handle, a hurdy-gurdy I fancy. My wife bent towards me and hissed, 'Or are you going to stay my bed husband, and know the friendship of my upper thighs? This hall has one of the finest hammerbeam roof-truss constructions in the county. It looks and is strong. This is put into that, you see. As above, so below . . .'

'You know I don't mind. It's your happiness I want.' Of course I was sincere about this. Not only because if she was not happy she would send out shock-waves on all channels so that it was impossible to remain calm in her vicinity, but because on those occasions when she was content it was like butter-moon shining; I mean, the whole world was right, because, happy, she was so *right*. I wasn't sure how happy she was now.

'Cost effective. Cost effective.' She was snapping her fingers and looking around her. In the flaming torchlight, in her heaped-up dress with the spreading white silk collar up to her ears, with her flunkeys and flatterers running around this way and that, I felt as if somebody had lit a November the fifth bonfire for children, and the effigy was restless and dancing on its poles, and the moths were gathering, though no flames were yet to be seen.

'I want to buy archers. I need revenues for defence. That blackbeard baron in the hills has his eye on this place. It would be an excellent alliance if I weren't married already.' The greeny-black major-domo shot me a glance. He had got hold of another poignard, and was cleaning his nails again. The heat in the corridor and the closeness of that stifling velvet gown, which looked at sleeves and neck as though it were stuffed with white radiance, was too much for me all of a sudden. I bent over the belling skirt and hissed back at her.

'Wife, I'm sleepy . . . so much to see . . .'

'Sleepy . . . I see . . .' Her grin told me that her upper thighs needed their friend. I only hoped that she would take the dress off.

She did. This time she did everything on top, and she wore a lacy frothy petticoat which hissed like the acid of the evil sea out of which this demesne had been conjured. Nor would she stop talking as she did it.

'I want the orchard thinned and those oaks in the south meadow can go, I don't care if they are older than the castle . . .' She then gave an enormous convulsion inside herself, great doors slammed open, and there was a twirling sensation like the barley-sugar pillars of her baldacchino porchway, and a gust of darkly scented hot air which must have been her sigh, but which came from her whole body. It was too much for me. I remembered nothing more . . .

. . . until the dawn light pearled the window. My extraordinary wife was still talking.

'And as I said to that black baron we'll have to define our boundaries again since good walls make good neighbours . . . oh is it dawn already, that's fine, I must get the carpenter to fit out those laying-sheds *tout de suite* . . . but I won't join up with those petty warring princelets and the only solution as I see it is for me to become king.' I was awake enough now to understand what she meant by this. I didn't like it one bit.

'King. So I want you to go down to the seashore and talk to that flounder of yours again and I'll see that it's made worth your while when you come back.'

'If I do come back. That flounder is a mighty power. He won't be pleased you're not content with what he's given you.'

'Not content? Of course I'm content. But I'm not the sort who stays at the bottom of the heap, am I? It's merely an adjustment, for him. That's not too much to ask, surely.'

All further agreement was drowned in a clatter of hooves. A groom had brought my horse to the very bedside. So it was not long before I was standing on the shore again.

The sea certainly looked worse. There was a black oily slick that must have been at least a mile square moving north with an undulant motion, like a giant ray. Where the slick ended, the green waves broke, and stank as they split. There were pieces of timber all over the foreshore, as if a lifeboat had broken up.

> 'Platichthys princeps, *princely fish,*
> *Rise like a god and grant my wish,*
> *Dick-headed through your briny sky,*
> *Grant my wish but don't ask why –*
> *Remember the Sunday I saved your life –*
> *If it ends in "day" I must please my wife.'*

A nearby portion of the rainbowing slick animated itself and revealed the outlines of the flounder. It had grown while I was away and was now the size, say, of a double bed. Flatfish have curiously twisted faces, on account of their starting out like ordinary fish, but then the eyes migrate so that one side gets both eyes and that's its face; the other side is now blind and is its belly. I thought of Quasimodo, or the Phantom of the Opera. Cultivated tones issued from the chaotic countenance.

'I know what she wants.'

'But she wants to be king!'

'She's crowned already.' I shrugged my shoulders and bowed as bigface sank below his rainbows in one enormous undulation.

I expected the bus to let me off at the castle stop, as before, but instead it turned left and began to climb. As we came over the rise I had a fine view of the hills flanking the lake with its islands and the snow-capped mountain behind. The foothills were now covered with buildings, and on the biggest of them flashed a golden roof. I was willing to bet that was hers. But then, all of it would be hers. There was a barrier across the road and a small ugly building like a customs shed. A laconic, pallid individual dressed for the part in a navy-blue uniform with brass buttons asked me for my exeat. He had to repeat his question as I was staring hypnotised at his buttons. Stamped on each one was a picture of my wife, crowned, naked, and on a rearing horse. She brandished a sword in one hand and a bearded severed head in the other. I pulled my eyes away from this sinister reminder of the neighbouring baron.

'I don't need an exeat. I am the Prince Consort.' I was getting used to these situations. The tall boy in the buttons lifted a phone, spoke for a moment looking at me all the time, put the phone down and disappeared behind his shed. A moment later he came back wheeling a golden bicycle with a small crown bolted to the handlebars. I was expected this time.

An onshore wind helped me make short work of the journey. There was a rack of bicycles of various colours at the foot of the principal hill and I left mine in a space labelled 'Prince Consort'. I began to climb the marble steps up the hill, and it was as though one of our ordinary little village streets had been transposed to marble halls of dazzling white. It was absolutely inappropriate. There was a green-grocer whose stock of oranges and plums were laid out on artificial turf thrown over wooden fruit-boxes. His posters of rosy children munching into apples rosier than themselves hardly made an impression on the airy marble pavilion where he had taken up his trade. Three shivering cashiers and a black-suited bank manager attended to their clients from behind a counter dwarfed by the dome under which they shivered, which struck very cold as the sun did not penetrate these tight-packed buildings, and the white marble cast cold dank shadows. A newsagent sold coloured journals from the margin of what looked and felt like an ice-rink, for a cold wind blew from it. I kept climbing towards the gold roof. Since this was the pinnacle of the town, I wondered whether it would be freezing from the mountain breezes, or roasting from the sun beating down on the precious metal dome.

The porch this time was Palladian, with the tall straight fluted pillars throwing a labyrinth of shadows. With the increased altitude, it seemed that the baroque barley-sugars had straightened themselves to respectability. The great dome behind the portico gave out a tone of echo even before you stepped into it, and this I knew was intentional in all such buildings, and its function was to increase awe by mere vibration. I stepped under the coffered orb and was confronted by an immense snow-white madonna with a tiny distant pink face. It took me a moment or two to overcome the illusion produced by the sight of my wife in white robes and sitting on a marble throne. I had taken the thirty feet of steps as an extension of her gown. I realised why no petrol engines were allowed past the customs barrier. It was to keep the air pure, so that the marble should not be stained, for it was her emblem. As I watched, men in robes of green and black passed to her various items of regalia, which she held a moment, raising them up to show to the people (who could not be called a crowd in that vast space); there were about a thousand subjects dotted over the floor and standing respectfully. The last object was a golden crown with some kind of indistinct appendage attached. This she held above her, and then adjusted on her head. Attached to the crown was a full beard-and-whisker set, which settled about her face and made her look like the Bearded Venus at the Circus. It seemed logical; how could she be called the king otherwise? I thought I should make myself visible, so I began mounting the stairs. She smiled at me, and beckoned. I paused on the final step; I thought it prudent to kneel. I heard the whistling of her skirts as she came down and lifted me up, and in the full view of that assembly she hugged me and gave me a whiskery kiss. There was loud and prolonged applause which cracked round the dome like the sound of electricity. She sat me down on the step and resumed her throne. A terrible cold from the marble began to penetrate my jeans and attack my scrotum. I hoped that if I stayed I would get some new clothes. I wondered if I would be here longer than a night this time.

There was a fanfare. She raised her arms in blessing, and turned, gathering her superstructure around her, and began walking down the stairs at the back of the throne. The effect on the crowd must have been like a snow-white penis retracting into its foreskin. I scurried after. I found her in a robing-room. Male servitors in green and black were hanging up her white dress. I noticed they all carried small poignards. She was wearing a woollen vest and pantaloons. She threw herself in an armchair and lit a small cigar. As the fragrance of the tobacco filled the room, I realised that throughout my journey into this land there had until this moment been no odours. Nothing smelt. Then she started rabbiting on and I felt thoroughly at home again.

A green-eyed servitor gently removed the crown from her head and the whiskers came with it. She opened her arms to me, and the loving merciless tirade continued.

I woke to it, in the dazzle of a white bed in a room the size of Waterloo Station. I thought I was still sleeping as my eyes could find no resting-place. It was like the effect the psychologists produce by sealing the two halves of a ping-pong ball over your eye-sockets; they call it a *ganzfeld*. Then I focused on the radical black crackle of my wife's hair spread across her pillow, and, in the centre of this web, the dark hole of her mouth opening and shutting like a spider busy eating an invisible fly.

'Of course I'm happy. But that doesn't mean everything is perfect. In fact it's a fiddling irritation that I can't pull more rank over these other kings. Why don't you go back to the flounder and tell him to make me emperor? That'd solve everything.'

'Why don't you come too? Then you could explain exactly what you wanted.'

'What! With a whole kingdom to run? So far as I'm concerned it's your job to call up spirits from the vasty deep. After all, you do it so well.'

At that she got on top of me, and the great nether door in her opened and closed in that enormous undulation which resembled nothing so much as the flounder's mode of locomotion. Though, as I said before, it was also like architecture. Romanesque, with its pillared vestibule expanding into a dome through which coffered panels shunted like trains, and a blazing white throne with a face rose to meet me. Ah, it's so difficult to describe sex . . .

That's how I found myself on the shore again in the early morning. I was very doubtful about this one. You can annexe lands and run elaborate buildings up very rapidly, but it is no simple matter to disappear existing emperors. The sea was black this time, like molasses, and there were large heaving swells which broke slowly, but broke white, like Guinness. There was a smell like neither molasses nor Guinness, but more like shit frying with onions, and it beat in pulses as the heavy swells shattered.

> 'Platichthys princeps, *principal fish,*
> *Rise from your chasms and grant my wish,*
> *Prick your head through your nether sky,*
> *I must plead again, and you know why,*
> *Remember, on Sunday I spared your life,*
> *So help me now to please my wife.'*

The flounder had grown so much that I was not aware of it until one of the long black waves reared and out of its under-chasm came a cultured voice and a sweet air tingling with seaside ozone. I looked for the eyes; they were floating a couple of hundred yards out and I had taken them for yellow-painted mooring buoys.

'I know what she wants before you ask.'

'How can she be emperor!'

'She already is.'

'Well, thank you, flounder, for impossibilities.'

The new ring road made it possible for the bus to approach the city via the river valley. I saw that in a few hours my wife had extended her former capital over the great lake's seven islands, and skyscrapers reared against the shadowy slopes of the mountain. The roads were very busy, and I noticed many eagles. These birds cluster around emperors as flies around carrion. We drew up by an immense façade of black glass. People hurried in and out of self-opening doors. A commissionaire in a bottle-green tailcoat and a black topper emerged and stood by the bus's doorway, and uncovered as I descended. I passed through into a great plaza with many lifts the size of small dining-rooms ascending and descending in transparent tubes. The principal smell was bay-rum and Chanel *Joie de vivre* which mingled with the clip-clop and tick-tock of hurrying footwear into a synaesthetic insight that time was money. I was put into a lift like a floating boardroom with a long shiny table and blotters and whisked up two hundred storeys as if I were the Chairman of the Board ascending to heaven. More doors slid open. There was my wife coming to meet me from behind a desk large and shiny as an Olympic pool among oak-panelling like a slaughtered forest. She was wearing a charcoal-grey three-piece suit with a golden watch and chain across the waistcoat and an Old Etonian tie.

'Good to see you, husband. I'm emperor.'

'I can see.'

'I have kings in committee.'

'So long as you're happy.'

'I will be happy when I have discharged my responsibilities. These are not purely secular, you know. Not just a matter of services, revenues, taxes.' She stuck her thumbs in her waistcoat pockets and played scales on her belly. 'There are things beyond all that.'

'True enough.'

'I'm glad you understand.' Arpeggios. 'There is a power beyond us all to which we are all subject.'

'Amen.'

'That's why I want to be pope.'

'That means . . .'

'Exactly. Back to the flounder.'

'At once? Time is money.'

'Not immediately . . .' and with a quick flick of her white-cuffed wrist her dark hair fell loose over the charcoal-grey shoulders. It seemed I was to be laid by the Imperial Chairperson of all, on her boardroom carpet soft as moss and among the mutilated oaks: as if she were the goddess of the butchered grove of panelling. The goddess removed her trousers and carefully hung them on the back of a chair. I lost consciousness as something like a print-out machine inside her chattered out an exceptional balance-sheet of golden transactions. I heard her crying out 'Your Holiness! Your Holiness!' and all was blank.

I didn't really come to until I noticed that the green-eyed chauffeur was holding open the door of the Rolls and inviting me to alight for the seashore. I found that I had acquired a charcoal-grey uniform identical to the chairperson's, and the pockets were stuffed with portraits of Florence Nightingale each worth ten pounds. I handed one to the driver, who tipped his forefinger to his cap ironically. I found myself in a winter landscape.

Leaves were blowing off the trees, and it was getting dark already. The waves were marching in like squads of gigantic dragoons with feathery plumes on their helmets. There was a trailing light in the sky and three distinct thumps; it was the maroon calling the lifeboat out to the rescue – a ship must be sinking somewhere out of sight – oh the poor mariners in such a sea. And there was more where that came from, with the clouds scudding so fast, and great black and purple thunderstorms massing on the horizon. It was like the end of the world; a nuclear winter. I could hardly make my way down to the beach, except by leaning on the wind with my head turned; the gusty air kept on tugging my breath away.

I got as near to the sea's margin as I could; every wave as it drew back and reared to its elephant-height sucked deep abysses down to the shingle and beyond, so I could see deep into the sea where cottage-sized boulders rolled. I wondered how ever the flounder was going to hear me in this racket or even get close to the shore.

Then the wind dropped, and I heard a still, small voice:

'Homo sapiens, *sapient soul,*
You saved my life, I was in a hole
But am mighty again; I will grant your wish;

The Flounder

You saw through my floundership; I was not a mere fish;
When men believe, it gives us hope.
I will grant your plea; your wife is pope.'

I looked for the flounder. He was nowhere to be seen. Unless he
was the whole sea. Two orange-coloured clouds high up that could
have been his eyes were being covered over by the resuming blackness.
I said 'Thank you' very loudly and began making my way back up the
beach; almost flew now the wind was with me.

This time I found a crowd of priests waiting for me, hunched over
candles they were keeping alight under their capes, and chanting.
They looked like crow-coloured trouble to me. Was this her Inquisition? Would they accuse me of consorting with sea-devils? How I
wished I were that seagull there, diving on the wind into the great
cloud, unharmed however black it was, bathing in the inexhaustible
fountains and in the lightnings unscorched; soaring above to the
stratospheric labyrinths and through the snowy organ-lofts which
create the thunder, the blowy mazes, and the cities of ice-castles and
frozen floating electrostatic water-machines. Ah well, back to earth. I
went up to the most important-looking priest, and bowed. To my
surprise, he bowed back.

'What do you want of me?' I asked.

'To invest you as cardinal and escort you to Her Holiness.' Two
priests were struggling with a scarlet cape that they put round my
shoulders and two others with a great round hat the same colour,
looking heavy as a harvest moon. I felt I would blow away in these
sail-like garments, but the sturdy young celibates lifted me by the
shoulder, waist and legs and carried me running towards a white
Popemobile that was waiting for us on the upper road.

We drove past the capital city and past the Imperial lake-islands.
What was that building white as snow on the distant peak of the
mountain? We stopped at the foot of the mountain and my escort
bowed me into the gold and white cable-car waiting there. The
funicular rose humming into the mountain breezes. I felt very excited
by this exaltation of my wife, for she must be waiting for me in the
vatican of ice at the end of the cable.

Perhaps it was the air, but I felt quite drunk as I stepped out on to
the platform and saw the immense view spread before me. This
skyscraper city was hers; these splendid plazas and porticoes; it was
hers as far as I could see – no, correction, there was a glimpse of the

white-ridged stormy sea; that was not hers. But this whole mountain with its lakes and fertile winterlands was; and here on the peak of it she, our pope, communed with her God. Tipsy with the thin air, I saw the whole thing quite clearly. Her task was urgent, to turn the world into its proper courses before it was too late. As I entered the snowy halls I saw my own sin; it was I who should have changed, with her, to keep her company. It must be so lonely being pope. I would rehearse proper words of confession in her service. I would sing them aloud so she could hear my heart opening out like a snow-flower in the cold air. And so I walked the ice-cold oxygen-thin corridors chanting my love song to my transfigured wife.

> *'The race of men has become violent and sinful,*
> *It has failed to perceive deity*
> *In the feminine principle.*
> *Due to the limited intelligence of men*
> *And their lust in this age called by seers*
> *The Kali Yuga, the said males are totally impotent*
> *To recognise women as direct manifestations*
> *Of the Shakti, of the Shakti, the Shaaaakti.'*

Then I heard a thin high voice far off chanting in return:

> *'Very few, only a very few, the manly few,*
> *Only they escape the combustion and destruction,*
> *The few, the only few, who are dedicated*
> *To the lotus of their mother's feet*
> *And the Yonis of their wives.'*

I had come out into a dazzling domed concourse like the Albert Hall painted white. My cardinal's trailing robes looked like a chainsaw massacre committed over that floor. At the back of the hall, where the organ would have been if it were the Albert Hall, a pulpit the size of a small church writhed with all the animals and races in creation, as though carved in snow. I saw my wife's face hovering at the summit. I could not this time tell whether the whole castellated pulpit was not her new popish garment. I called out.

'You are so high up, my dear, that your voice has gone thin.'

'That is my holy voice, dearest. Thin and entuned through the nose, because God does not use mouths to speak with. I will descend.'

I wondered whether this would not take a long time, but I heard a swishing noise and I realised that she had a sleigh and a papal Cresta Run down to ground level. I helped her out. She was wearing a simple white soutane. A close-fitting skull-cap concealed her black hair. She spoke first.

'Those who ascend the papal pulpit beyond the mountain's tip must use the holy voice due to the air's rarefaction. It is the angel's voice.' She looked me up and down. 'I am very glad you came back.' This surprised me. How could I not come back! 'At last my work is beginning to show some fruit.'

'Then you're happy?' That would be the best reward for all my errands to the abyss.

'Happy?' She ruminated the word. 'It is no sinecure looking after the works of God. I so often feel that I shall always lack something of the eternal insight; and I certainly lack God's unequalled capacity to depute necessary tasks. Look – the sun is setting and I haven't even finished my prayers yet. And then there's us . . .'

'I thought popes were celibate.'

'Not female ones. And you are only a cardinal.' She moved closer, and kissed me. To an observer it would have looked like a snow-woman nibbling a blood-clot. I was quite stunned by the kiss. There was holiness in her lips, all right. Then she spoke again.

'If only I could stop the sun to give me more time . . .'

I grasped her meaning immediately.

'Now, my dear . . .' It was as far as I got.

'Come to think of it, I wouldn't have to pray so hard either if I were . . .' she went on.

'Don't say it,' I whispered.

'God,' said my wife. I felt something moving under my feet. It was probably an earth-tremor.

'Did you feel that! It'll be avalanches and earthquakes; your wonderful city and all your people will be destroyed if you blaspheme so, my love.'

'You have to go back and tell the flounder. I can't bear it any longer. I must be God. I will be God, and hold the sun and the moon tightly in my hands.'

'Won't you come with me, to ask the flounder? He can explain impossible's impossible.'

'Go little man. Go this instant.' That upset me. But I judged it better to go. What about my nooky? I had missed it this time. But if she were successful, next time I would be having it with – God.

I don't know how I got down that funicular. The cable-car was blowing on its cable like a priest swinging a thurible among clouds of snow-flurry. The Popemobile was waiting for me, and several times we had to stop and I helped lift fragments of masonry from the road. I saw a tremendous snow-white statue of my wife crumble as a shock-wave under the paving hit it. I expected the road to open up into chasms at any moment, and our Holiness-car to drive straight into the smoking depths. The thunder sounded like the tearing of rocks in the sky and the rain came down like bars of a steel cage shaken by invisible dinosaurs. 'We must drive fast,' I called out to the chauffeur who was wearing a cassock so old it had gone bottle-green, 'if we are to forestall global destruction.'

But it was all quiet at the beach. The clear water lapped gently at the band of seaweed and other jetsam thrown up by the storm. The air was clean and fresh. I felt awe in the quiet as I made my way over the shingle. I stood watching the gentle water and tasting the salt air on my lips for a while before I made my prayer.

> *'Flounder, flounder, magical fish,*
> *I saved your life, so grant my wish,*
> *My wife is tearing the world apart,*
> *So give her what is close to her heart,*
> *For all our sakes, fish. She wants to be God.'*

Nothing. Was it the beginning of the end, then, this quiet that gave back no answer? Then I saw a feeble movement among the stalks and broad straps of seaweed at my feet. I knelt and cleared some of the litter away. It was the flounder, small again, looking very flat, with patches of skin missing, and its corkscrew face agonised, the eyes glazing. It was like nothing so much as a foetus aborted by the waves. There was another small hopping movement as the fringed tail flapped. I lifted it up. It wriggled slightly in my hand. I bent my head to its mouth. 'My friend, your wish is granted,' it said, and died.

I walked into the sea up to my waist and held it in my palm under the water, but it did not come to life and swim away again as I had hoped. I turned my hand over and it fell away through the water, out of sight. I felt grief, but also peace. The temptation to wish for more and more upon more had gone. Unless – unless my wife had become God after all, despite the flounder's death.

I climbed up the beach. The road had disappeared, swallowed up by a last convulsion of the earthquake, no doubt. I could see no trace of the city in the distance. Our old ruined barn where we used to sleep in the big manger was back again, however. A single bright star had risen, twinkling directly above our old home. Well, I thought to myself, we've at least got a roof over our heads. And there was my wife coming to meet me, dressed as she always used to dress, with her shawl round her shoulders and her hair in a bun and her skirt held up in a knot to her belly. I speeded up because I was lonely for the old days, and wanted to hug her. What she said as I came close made me want to hug her all the more.

'Lover, I'm pregnant again.'

The Master-thief

The Master-thief

Never and never, my girl riding far and near
In the land of the hearthstone tales, and spelled asleep,
Fear or believe that the wolf in a sheepwhite hood
Loping and bleating roughly and blithely shall leap,
                    My dear, my dear,
Out of a lair in the flocked leaves in the dew dipped year
To eat your heart in the house in the rosy wood.

'If you had planted our beans straight this year, Ertha, I could have rested after work and enjoyed their vistas narrowing to the borders of our self-sufficiency, our smallholding. As it is, you have made a witch's labyrinth of those bean-rows.' The old man is in rags, but his gold spectacles glint on his nose like determined principles. His wife is a dwarf.

'You can't tell where they end then, can you? Our garden is a labyrinthine fractal and therefore infinite.' The old man, Ian, does not reply. He is staring over the low stone wall.

'There's a black carriage magnificent as a king's hearse coming up the lane. It'll break its wheels on our terrain. Four black stallions, no less! Why here? We lead nowhere. He'll want a glass of water, Ertha.'

'I'll pump him one, Ian.' The dwarf toddles down the crooked bean-rows to their tumbledown cottage.

'It can't be tourism, or a desire to taste our simple unspoiled country food,' says Ian to himself. 'Not with all that prance and gold and black. Why, the passenger is in gold and black too. Good morning, My Lord. How may we serve you?' The old man bows obsequiously to the tall athletic figure with the Basil Rathbone nose.

'What a delightful spot!' the new arrival observes. 'What beautiful air! My good old man, I am here for nothing but to taste simple unspoiled food.'

'Unspoiled food?'

'Yes. I want you to cook me some potatoes the way you cook them for yourselves, and I want to sit down with you and eat and enjoy them as if I were a member of your household. Coachman! Drive the carriage around the corner so it's out of sight!'

'Simple food.'

'That's right. Earth-apples.'

'You must be used to gourmet menus. We could do you a nice Boeuf Bourginon.'

'No, no, no. Potatoes. Just as you eat them.'

'We are very fond of Boeuf Bourginon.'

'I am not one of your ordinary tourists, you know.'

'I know, My Lord, that you must be a count or a duke or an earl, and I am confident such honourable folk have their fancies.'

'I have brought some wine for my contribution.' They sit down, and the visitor produces a bottle and two pewter mugs.

'Now, that's better. Would you like to see our garden? We are self-sufficient, you know. I would like to dig another of these holes for the fruit trees before supper.'

'I will help you.'

'You sir? No. You are our guest.'

'It is my fancy. I would like to be more than a guest. Give me the shovel.' The black and gold visitor plies the spade like a master.

'That's good, sir, very good. You might have been born to it.'

'Why have you no children? You call yourself self-sufficient, but where are your children to help you work? You cannot rely on passing strangers.'

'We had a son, sir, but it was bitterness for me and Ertha, my wife. He was what you call a hyperactive child. Never still, always bouncing about with schemes and mischief of all sorts. He was clever and sharp, but such a one for the girls, and never respected school-learning. He ran away from home in the end. We never heard of him again. Let me just plant this tree, sir, in the hole that you've made. See, I put a stake of wood in beside it, and tamp the earth down well with my hands. Now with this straw I must tie the stem to this stake above and in the middle and below, so it will not grow crooked.'

'That tree over there, that's knotted and crooked so that it is almost a shrub, crawling over the ground, can't you straighten that by tying it to a stake?'

'No, sir. You have to train them when they are young. Nothing will ever make that tree straight. Nothing.'

'I am thinking about your son, old man. If you'd trained him and brought him up straight while he was young, then he would not have run away.'

'It's true, My Lord. How many years it is since then! He must be quite changed.'

'Would you know him, if he stood here, in your garden?'

'His face, I daresay, would not tell me, but I'd know him by the birthmark on his shoulder, something like a bean in shape.'

'Is it like this mark on my shoulder?'

'Oh, My Lord. It can't be! Are you my son?' Ian is dancing about like a child. 'Ertha, Ertha, quick, come here. Our son has returned.'

The dwarf appears round the corner of a bean-row. Among the tall plants she looks as small as a bird. She notices the men already have their drinks and mugs, so she carefully pours the water she is carrying on to the roots of a bean. 'What son?' she says at last.

'Your child!' The dwarf looks up sharply, and hobbles towards them. She is quick on the uptake.

'My child, my baby? My son? How can you be! Let me feel you with my hands. You are a great gentleman. You are. You live in the midst of wealth and drive a black carriage with black horses like Death himself. My son?'

'You mustn't fear what life brings, Mother.'

'I lost my son and I lost my second child, your sister. How can I be other than afraid? And now you come back and expect me to be grateful. How did you get all that wealth, anyway?'

'You are right, dear parents. The young tree was not properly trained. It has grown crooked, and it is now too late to straighten it. I have been a thief all my life, but you must not worry about my profession.'

'One child a thief and the other a sleeping beauty.' The dwarf is weeping now. Her husband looks at her emotion inquisitively with his sharp nose and valuable glasses.

'What do you mean, Mother. My sister? I had expected she was married, and you would tell me where she was.'

Ian speaks without emotion. 'No, it was after you left home. We could not wake her one morning. I went in with her hot tea and there she was in bed as usual and so deeply asleep and so beautiful I couldn't believe my eyes, and I thought that with such beauty, what would the first words be that she uttered this morning of fine sunshine, they would be religious words that would help us all, I was sure. But she would not wake. Not then or ever after. She would not wake.'

'Can I see her?' asks the black and gold self-confessed thief.

'Your godfather, the count in the castle where I was tutor in those days, took pity on her. He has nurses taking care of her day and night in a special room that is guarded against anyone who might want to steal her beauty away. He loves beautiful things above all, as only an ugly man can.'

'She is my sister, I should take care of her myself.'

'The count, he wouldn't hear of it. Why, we ourselves are scarcely allowed to see her. Never more than once a year. And though you seem like a great lord, you are a thief, by your own admission.'

'Father, I am a master-thief.'

'Well, what does that mean, if anything?'

'It means quite simply that if anything takes my fancy, nothing can withstand my stealing it. Not locks or bolts or soldiers or guards, no persuasion or poetry, no reason or rhyme, no magic or monster. That is what it means to be a master-thief.'

'I don't care for it, son. A thief is a thief. And a thief comes to a bad end.'

'But I will see my sister, whatever the count says. And maybe steal her away with me. It is certain I can wake her, for Death is the only thing that can stand against a master-thief. Death is the greatest thief of them all, Death steals everything, the master-criminal; and when the master-thief joins with Death then all must look out. Moreover, my badness is so extreme that it turns to goodness; so sure am I of my craft that I scorn to steal from any but the rich. I help myself to their abundance, and return the superflux to the poor after I have taken my expenses. I am, like Death my teacher, the great equaliser.'

'Though you are a thief, and whatever all your high talk signifies, you are my son and I rejoice to see you; these old eyes run with living water. I still say that when His Lordship finds out you're a thief, godfather or no, he'll not rock you in his arms as he did at your christening, he will rock you instead on his own castle gallows.'

'He can't hurt me. I know my trade better than any man. I will go to the count of the castle today. But first let us eat. Jump up, little mother!'

The dwarf, smiling now, clambers into the master-thief's arms. 'You always liked potatoes,' she says, and kisses him.

> *Under the prayer wheeling moon in the rosy wood*
> *Be shielded by chant and flower and gay may you*
>
> *Lie in grace. Sleep spelled at rest in the lowly house*
> *In the squirrel nimble grove, under linen and thatch*
> *And star: held and blessed, though you scour the high four*
> *Winds, from the dousing shade and the roarer at the latch,*
> > *Cool in your vows.*
> *Yet out of the beaked, web dark and the pouncing boughs*
> *Be you sure the Thief will seek a way sly and sure*
>
> *And sly as snow and meek as dew blown to the thorn,*
> *This night and each vast night until the stern bell talks*
> *In the tower and tolls to sleep over the stalls*
> *Of the hearthstone tales my own, lost love; and the soul walks*
> > *The waters shorn.*

The lean black and gold visitor is pacing up and down. Count Bast, the ruler, regards him jovially from his state chair.

'The schedule of the law you passed, My Lord, said "anyone". Anyone who succeeds in the three tasks to be specified by Your Lordship may marry your god-daughter. His last and additional task is to wake her. If you did not want your godson to compete, then you should have said so. With respect.'

Bast laughs. 'As you admit to being a master-thief, maybe I should hang you first, and make that one of your tasks: to get out of the marriage with the ropemaker's daughter.'

The Rathbone look-alike stops pacing and looks hard at Bast. 'As you please, My Lord.'

'Well, I think it would be more interesting to watch your antics over the tasks already set, for if you cannot complete them, then I will hang you anyway.'

'And if I do complete them?'

'You shall marry my god-daughter.'

'It was you who decreed that brother–sister marriages were against the law.'

'So they are, but if you succeed in my difficult tasks I shall consider the marriage confirmed by heaven. However, the lady may have other views when she wakes.'

The master-thief smiles his amazing smile. 'Give me your tasks. Remember, a master-thief is merely a catalyst.'

'Number one. Steal my best horse out of its stable. It is my mount as commander-in-chief. I am head of the army by its virtue. Its name is General Starlight. My commands in the field are obeyed only if I ride this horse or its lineage.'

'I shall steal your Starlight.'

'Next. After the countess and I have retired for the night, steal both the sheet from under us and the wedding-ring off my wife's finger.'

'That is intimate but not difficult. Not for a master-thief.'

'Last. Steal the archbishop and his chaplain out of their church.'

'I shall certainly have to steal them away if I am to marry my illegal sister–bride in their legitimate church.'

'You are the master-thief. Thieve on,' twinkled Bast.

Ever and ever he finds a way, as the snow falls,

As the rain falls, hail on the fleece, as the vale mist rides
Through the haygold stalls, as the dew falls on the wind-
Milled dust of the apple tree and the pounded islands
Of the morning leaves, as the star falls, as the winged
        Apple seed glides,
And falls, and flowers in the yawning wound at our sides,
As the world falls, silent as the cyclone of silence.

The master-thief strolls through the red-light district. He wants to play some strip-poker. He stops at a particularly tacky-looking pub, and enters. It is not long before he is sitting down with a gang of assorted villains who seem to know one another. At first they think he's easy meat. They are soon dissuaded.

'There you are, Mother Fritello, a straight flush. Another of your garments, please. I think that filthy, really filthy petticoat should do.'

It's a good job none of the customers is fussy. Old Mother Fritello sitting there topless with her dugs swinging to her waist wouldn't pull in your average casual customer.

'Full house!' cries the master-thief to the glum crone. She has now lost all her clothes. The innkeeper, nervous at the turn events have taken, comes across and stokes up the fire, for the benefit of the nude old woman. 'I'll play you for your wrinkles now, shall I?' crows the master-thief. 'You've lost everything else!'

The innkeeper at the bar wishes that the dark visitor would be more tactful about his good luck. As a stranger, he probably doesn't realise the situation he's in. If he keeps on winning, he'll lose. The old woman and her four sons – Mother Fritello, Fricasso, Cocodrillo, Fritellino and Captain Cerimonia – will simply cut his throat and take everything.

'Friends, I think I have everything now,' says the master-thief. 'I feel I am sitting with five corpses, naked in the firelight. I am the only living one since I am the only one clothed.'

'We'll bet you our bodies. Our souls too, if we could find them.' Fritellino is sullen.

'That cask you are sitting on, Cocodrillo. What is that?'

'Quite empty, My Lord,' lies Cocodrillo.

'Just shake it for me, will you. What is that gurgling?'

'Oh that.'

'Yes, that gurgle,' twinkles the master-thief.

Mother Fritello intervenes. 'It's our living, sir. The very best Hungarian wine that we water down and sell to the soldiers. Not worth your attention, worthy sir.'

'The soldiers know you all, do they? And that bundle of herbs you have just kicked into the shadows, Cerimonia. Is that something else you sell to the soldiers? Ah ha, I think I know this kind of grass. Tuscan, isn't it? Finest Tuscan.' The master-thief is talking fast. He has got them where he wants them.

'Reputed to have given that poet – what's-his-name – Durante Alighieri – his visions of heaven and hell,' continues the master-thief. Bland Cerimonia, for once, can find no words. Dogged Fricasso fumes, decides diplomacy is the best way. This commanding stranger is an unknown quantity, though he does have a throat, like everybody else. 'It transforms soldiers to angels. Mother dances like a houri for them, and they fall in love,' he says.

The master-thief keeps the pressure on. 'Double or quits, then. Cut for it all.'

'Done,' says the gang.

'You are done. You can't even cut my throat now, can you? I've got your knives.'

'I can strangle you with my bare hands.' The giant Fritellino starts to get up.

'But I am the master-thief, Fritellino. Here are your goods, all of them, and gold besides, if you will be my gang.'

'Gang to the master-thief! It is the equivalent of apprenticeship to a great artist!' They are all amazed. But a master-thief! That explains everything. They were putty in his hands, and that is nothing to be ashamed of, not with a master-thief. Only the old woman is sullen because she feels cold.

'Gimme my clothes.'

'No, no, old woman, you shall have mine.'

'Your clothes, master-thief?' This man never ceases to amaze.

'It is time for you to strip me. Go on, now. Take all my clothes. It is warm enough here. Take off, that's right, the breeches, the shirt. Now I am naked in the firelight – it is like being a boy again!'

The landlord can only see that murder has receded and skin games are commencing. He wants them to retire to the upstairs bedrooms as is usual. He begins to make signs, and is astonished when the gang glares at him. 'Go away, landlord. It's all working out fine for everybody,' says the master-thief, turning back to his horrible five. They are entranced. What is he up to now? 'These oak-galls on the firewood, pluck them off, and crush them under your boot and mix them with ashes on the hearthstone, and pour on a little of the sour wine – thus you have ink. Now take twigs like pens and, look old Granny, hold your face by mine, that's it – now you, draw upon my face all the wrinkles you see on Granny's, and on my hands and neck and chest, be a close artist, draw on me the portrait of age, that's it, it dries quickly, now help me put on her clothes. Ugh, they seem to wriggle as I put them on. Yes, all her petticoats, how shall I keep warm otherwise, this is master-thief's work. Aha, it is right, absolutely right. Yes, wear my man's clothes, Granny, if you want, and my rapier if you know how to use it.'

Granny, looking like an aged nobleman in the master-thief's clothes, draws the rapier with a swish of steel and rapidly runs through the eight basic postures of fencing. The master-thief himself now looks older than Granny ever did. He is puffing Cerimonia's long clay pipe, and looks on approvingly.

'That is fine, you can fight for us all. Right, give me that grass, I will steep it in the Hungarian wine. How is my walk, do I look like Granny in these clothes? Why, in mine, she hops and skips like a gallant. How about the cough, now – that's it,' he summons up a formidable phlegm and projects it into the fire, where it explodes like a whip-crack. 'Now, off to His Lordship's stables.'

> *Yet out of the beaked, web dark and the pouncing boughs*
> *Be you sure the thief will seek a way sly and sure*
>
> *And sly as snow and meek as dew blown to the thorn,*
> *This night and each vast night until the stern bell talks*
> *In the tower and tolls to sleep over the stalls*
> *Of the hearthstone tales my own, lost love; and the soul walks*
> *The waters shorn.*

'Hey, that's good wine, give me another glass,' calls a young soldier with a wonderful veined carbuncle on his nose.

'Take it for free. It's my birthday. Go on.' The master-thief, immersed in his part, cackles like a dotard.

'How old is that then, two hundred?' A second soldier, short, dark, weasely, is on guard in the courtyard.

'Cheeky! Drink up, my lad, then take another look. Cocodrillo, Fricasso, play the drum and the little pipe.'

'Oh, that's strange, I could have sworn you had wrinkles, but your face is young. Love me then, come close.'

'What will your comrades think?'

'They will want to love you too . . .' The youth with the mineralogical nose calls out to his comrades in the stable, 'Hey boys, this wine is free! We'll take some in for those on horse-duty. Let's have a real party.'

'Let them come out here,' insists the old-young master-drag-thief, 'We can dance in the courtyard.'

'They'll dance their lives away if they let go of that horse, His Lordship's marvellous horse,' says the weasel, 'but that's their responsibility. We look after the outer yard, so beware, old woman!' As he speaks, the soldier's legs are lowering him helplessly to the ground.

'I will,' says the old woman, 'let me just fold your cape and tuck it under your head, brave soldier.'

Carbuncle too is overwhelmed by the dancing and the drugged wine. 'You go in, old houri-mother, I feel so sleepy, I'll just take forty winks. Before the party.'

The master-thief, satisfied that his victims will snore on for several hours, tiptoes into the splendid stable. Cocodrillo and Fricasso follow with the snare-drum and the little pipe, beating time almost inaudibly. Like a bronze of heroic cavalry in the half-light, three soldiers are motionless and in attendance on a great black stallion splashed with white dapple, like constellations. One soldier sits astride the horse Starlight, another holds his reins, and the third his tail.

'It's my birthday,' says the master-thief, 'have some wine.'

'We're not supposed to move,' says the one holding the reins, who is the sergeant.

'Or speak,' says the one astride.

'Or sleep,' says the one gripping the tail.

'Then drink without breaking your vows, my lovers,' cackles the master-thief, going from soldier to soldier with the wineskin under his arm like a bagpipe, filling their mouths with the irresistible wine until they sway.

'Hey, where's the tail . . . ?' It has dropped from the nerveless fingers of the youngest guard.

'Here you are, lad,' says the master-thief, putting a long bundle of straw into his hand.

'They'll hang me. I've dropped the reins!' says the sergeant.

'That's all right, Sarge, I've got his tail.'

'Here are the reins, Sergeant,' says the master-thief, handing him a bit of rope nailed to a wooden pillar.

'I'm falling, old mother,' cries the soldier on horseback.

'I'll catch you, young friend,' responds the master-thief, easing him astride a large barrel he has rolled near. 'All safe then, lads?'

'All safe, mother. Happy birthday!' they call out, no longer bronze but stoned. Stealthily the master-thief leads the command stallion out of the stable, accompanied almost inaudibly by Cocodrillo on the snare-drum and Fricasso on the little pipe. Out in the courtyard Starlight walks like a four-legged, star-maned portion of the starry sky above. The master-thief springs into the saddle and, with a wink to his companions, is off into the night.

The Master-thief

Dawn is touching the sky as the master-thief reins up outside Count Bast's mansion. Cupping his hand to his mouth, he shouts up to the Count's bedroom.

'Lordship! Lordship! Your horse is stolen. Your command is stolen.'

The noise is considerable. Count Bast appears at the window. It's the truth. The elegant black-clad figure of the master-thief straddles the marvellous state-horse.

'My horse! Starlight! I'll have those soldiers' heads,' shouts Bast. The figure on horseback shakes a reproving finger.

'You will not have your horse again unless you pardon those soldiers. After all, they came up against a master-thief. How could they win? Pardon them, and your horse is stolen, and restored, and my first task done.'

Bast turns, and finds a colonel, his aide-de-camp, at his elbow.

'Your command-horse, My Lord. It's gone. The guards . . . they tried to pretend General Starlight was still in the stable – one pointed to some straw and said it was his tail, and the sergeant tried to rein him with an old rope fastened to a nail, while the third sat on a barrel and said how proud he was to have such a steed. Then he got off and began grooming the animal, and they all groomed the invisible body, and they are still doing it, laughing like madmen all the while. I hadn't the heart to strike their heads off while they were laughing. I wanted to see them groan for their crime. But I have reported to you immediately.'

'There it is,' says Bast grimly.

'Where?'

'In the street. With the master-thief riding. Oh, it's not your fault. What could even a colonel do against a master-thief.'

'The master-thief. Now I follow. No disgrace. They were only soldiers and I only a colonel. Against a master-thief.'

Fear most

> *For ever of all not the wolf in his baaing hood*
> *Nor the tusked prince, in the ruttish farm, at the rind*
> *And mire of love, but the Thief as meek as the dew.*

'Well, I'm not afraid of you.' Bast is leaning dangerously out of the window.

'Of course not,' says the master-thief.

'You seem to have discharged your first task.'

'I am gripping it between my knees.'

'I want to discuss your second, but do I have to shout it out of the window to the whole world?'

'I will come in.' The master-thief on horseback clatters past the porter who has just opened the gate. There is a noise of hooves on the stairs, and a cry of servants. The count's bedroom door flies open. 'There. I have brought Your Lordship's horse into Your Lordship's marriage chamber,' says the rider enthusiastically.

'I am glad that you have seen this room,' says Bast grimly, 'for remember your next task is to steal the sheet from my bed while I and Her Ladyship are lying on it, and the ring from Her Ladyship's finger, her marriage ring. I hope you will not find this too simple. I can see that, by using your imagination and a kind of hypnotic patter, you are able to misdirect people. I want to know your secrets, they would be useful to me. You seem to be able to create a panic around you, or a calm, as you please.'

'Would Your Lordship care to become my apprentice? My chief need is to visit my sleeping sister.'

'Tonight is Friday, which is called the Night of the Lord's Bedchamber. All married people must by law conjoin on Friday. It is forbidden they be disturbed by any matter whatsoever. The penalty is flaying. As feudal prince, I must lead in this custom. So you see, both the bedsheet and the marriage ring will be fully occupied.'

'As this is so propitious an eve, why was it that I saw all the condemned prisoners being shrived for execution as I rode here in the dawn? Why were all those ambulances out with their paramedical teams alert?' The master-thief pats General Starlight's neck, leaning forward in an attitude of earnest enquiry.

'It is also forbidden that on this day, which begins at twelve noon, there should be any death – again, on penalty of flaying – whether it be a doctor who allows his patient to die too early or too late, or a prison official charged with terminating a criminal. All outstanding capital sentences must be executed on this day. Many old people are put away before noon for this reason.'

'May I be forgiven if a mere master-thief considers this a barbarous custom?'

'The rites of the Death-Mother must not conflict with those of the Love-Goddess.'

'In my trade, they are the same lady, who is also the patron of thieves.'

'Then I trust she favours those who serve her best.'

'She does, sir, and always has.'

The country is holy: O bide in that country kind,
                    Know the green good,
Under the prayer wheeling moon in the rosy wood
Be shielded by chant and flower and gay may you

Lie in grace. Sleep spelled at rest in the lowly house
In the squirrel nimble grove, under linen and thatch
And star: held and blessed, though you scour the high four
Winds, from the dousing shade and the roarer at the latch,
                    Cool in your vows.

'Your ladyship forgive me. A passing fatigue.' The count holds a limp condom between finger and thumb.

'I suppose it was a passing fatigue on our wedding-night.'

'The drinks, the stag party . . . you've never forgotten that, have you?'

'Not when you remind me by being so . . .'

'Unmanly, is that what you mean? It happens to most men from time to time. What about *last* Friday?'

'Oh well, yes, that was grand. I'll give you that.'

'Oh, good. I feel *so* much better. To tell you the truth, Constance, I *am* worried about this so-called master-thief. He stands to win our god-daughter, and if he does so I shall have to ennoble him, into the bargain. I hate the idea of a master-thief, anyway – somebody who by a mere emphasis of his personality causes other people's goods to slide into his pocket. I don't want to leave it to the guards, either, since it's our bedsheet and your wedding-ring he's after. I can't help feeling that we will experience a sudden panic or delight that will enable him to steal in and win the bet. So as soon as I feel pleasure, it is punctuated by these thoughts.'

'I am feeling a sudden delight.'

'At the prospect of the master-thief entering our bedroom? It is his influence! He approaches somewhere . . .'

'What could he do while you are here, Rolly?' Countess Bast is snuggling up. She has rescued the condom from the bedside ashtray.

'If I remain alert . . .' Bast is priming a small pistol he has taken from a drawer. His lady holds out the condom.

'Prime your *other* pistol, my dear, come to bed . . .'

> *Never and never, my girl riding far and near*
> *In the land of the hearthstone tales, and spelled asleep,*
> *Fear or believe that the wolf in a sheepwhite hood*
> *Loping and bleating roughly and blithely shall leap,*
> > *My dear, my dear,*
> *Out of a lair in the flocked leaves in the dew dipped year*
> *To eat your heart in the house in the rosy wood.*

'So stop pacing up and down like that. Come to bed do.' Matters between them have gone from bad to worse. Bast feels his enemy's presence everywhere.

'It's his panic rising about us. I will not give in.'

'Oh, come to bed. Mind that gun doesn't go off at half-cock.'

'Listen!'

'What?'

'The scraping of a ladder on the wall.'

'Protect me, Rolly.'

'My gun's ready for him. I didn't think the master-thief would be that crude. There's his head rising above the sill. There, take that, you bastard!'

There is a sound like an exploding melon and the master-thief's head shatters. There is a slithering sound as the body falls back down the ladder.

'That's put a stop to his master-tricks. I'll call the guard.' Bast is jubilant.

'Rolly, it's Friday.'

'I know, dear. Where's the condom . . . ?'

'You shouldn't have killed him. On Friday.'

'Friday!'

'You'll be flayed, by your own law, for killing a man on Friday.'

'Oh my God. I shall have to sentence myself to death. Lodge an appeal to myself. Reject my own appeal on grounds of the evidence and hand myself over to the executioner.'

'There's only one thing you can do. You must bury the master-thief. In the garden.'

'Yes, yes, I will. I can see him from here. My shot blew the top of his head off. You lie still now, you villain. Such violence, such repose. I must make sure I have murdered my murderer. I'm going down. It will take time to dig a big enough hole.' Bast gingerly steps over the window-sill and descends the ladder. Almost immediately Countess Bast, who is still in bed, hears him returning.

'You're back soon.'

'Give me the sheet, wife.' Bast sounds a little subdued.

'The sheet, what for?'

'When I got down there I suddenly realised that he is, after all, our godson. I'd be burying him like a dog to put him as he is in the earth. I must wind him in one of our sheets.'

'Our silk bedsheets?'

'Yes, that will be good enough.'

'I should say so. I suppose you don't want anything else?'

'Look, he gave his life to get your ring. Be generous. Give it to him in death. I'll buy you another.'

'Our ring. Another . . . How could . . . ?'

'I feel guilty as hell about leading this poor man on. Give me the ring! It must go on his dead wedding-finger.'

'You'll get me another one . . .'

'Yes, yes, of course. I'm going down now.'

It seems no time at all has passed when Bast climbs in again. He looks grubbily cheerful. 'I need a bath now. What a night! I feel I've saved my skin.'

'Did you stow him safely, with my ring on his finger, wrapped nobly in silk like a lord?'

'Ring, sheet? What do you mean?' The jaws of Countess and Count Bast drop open simultaneously as they realise they've been had.

> *The stream from the priest black wristed spinney and sleeves*
> > *Of thistling frost*
> *Of the nightingale's din and tale! The upgiven ghost*
> *Of the dingle torn to singing and the surpliced*
>
> *Hill of cypresses! The din and tale in the skimmed*
> *Yard of the buttermilk rain on the pail! The sermon*
> *Of blood! The bird loud vein! The saga from mermen*
> > *To seraphim*
> *Leaping! The gospel rooks! All tell, this night, of him*
> *Who comes as red as the fox and sly as the heeled wind.*

'Here's the sheet. Here's the ring.' The master-thief lays them gently on Bast's desk.

'Do tell, Raffles. Do you simply create a magic panic round you? That's the countess's opinion. I swear I shot you on the ladder. Do you see the fineness of this sheet? I can draw it through the wedding-ring, thus. They would have drawn my skin off so. Can you create good dreams as well as nightmares?'

'I took a man from Thursday's gallows, and climbed up the ladder with him on my shoulders.' The master-thief studies his nails. 'You nearly shot both of us off the ladder. I knew you would want to kill me without bothering to think about it. Then when you were off burying the body in the rose bushes, I came up the ladder again, sounding like you in the shadows.' His voice changes to an exact replica of Bast's. 'I'd be burying him like a dog to put him as he is into the raw earth . . . You see.'

'I see. You are two-thirds of the way to marrying your sister. How will you perform the third task, I wonder? It is to steal the archbishop and his chaplain from the church.'

'I think that will be the easiest of all.'

'You haven't met the archbishop.'

The master-thief strides into the tavern where his gang are awaiting him.

'It's the big one, gang. I want you, Fricasso, to get me five hundred live crabs. I don't care where, just get them. Also, as you have an easy task, get as many candles. *Mère* Fritello, I want you to assemble in the great hall all the dressmakers in the town. Fritellino, here's gold. I want you to marshal the complement of the city's whores in the infant school. Your giant's stature will command obedience. Cocodrillo, will you steal silk from the great mercer's warehouse sufficient to clothe these whores? Now's the time to put to use what you have learnt from the master-thief, Cerimonia. Here's your costume. You are the visiting priest. You have come to get the archbishop to autograph his book for you.' Captain Cerimonia dons his soutane, biretta and steel-rimmed glasses and stands there, his great codpiece protruding from his priestly robes. 'Oh, take it off for once, Cerimonia,' grins the master-thief.

'I believe that all right-thinking people will be grateful to you, Arch-bishop, for this succinct compendium of the heresies. Not even your enemies have ever impugned your integrity; you are known in all councils as a man of your word. Your honest voice is needed now more than ever when the black tide of the occult, the sexual and the feminine is lapping at the very Church doors.'

Cerimonia, *sans* codpiece, the picture of celibate well-being, is holding forth in the library of the archbishop's palace. The prelate and his chaplain are unusually restless for clergymen. It is part of their new austerity to eat little, and to drink and smoke nothing.

'I am glad that you like my book, Father Cerimonia. It is the product of great experience. As priest and bishop.'

'It is both honest and timely. Would you not argue as an honest man and a priest of God that, should you encounter any of these phenomena, it would be incumbent on you to change your position?'

'All priests in this Church are celibate. Aren't we, chaplain?'

'I have the honour to be His Lordship's chaplain and to bear the name Chaplin. George Chaplin.' This comedian is a mousy priest with a purple bib. His hands are not steady. 'We are old friends, and stand together on these matters.'

'Indeed we are, George. Very celibate.' This, too, makes them restless, thinks Cerimonia, and suggestible. He is counting on it.

'And teetotal. It is the abuse of the senses by drugs, including tobacco . . .' Chaplin pauses; his face shines in a Father Brown smile '. . . alcohol and sexuality, which lead to the delusions My Lord has castigated. We are steady as a rock, and on the rock stands a lighthouse to guide all the souls into harbour. We have established by decree of Count Bast and inspiration of the Church that intercourse is to occur but once a week, on Friday, and that at night, so that the excited senses of the partners may be occupied only with dreams, and not realities, and they will awake refreshed to their usual occupations. Nevertheless we have a prostitution problem.'

Cerimonia pretends to be piqued. He knows what is coming. 'But there are faculties of the soul, as you yourself say, spiritual senses which are developed by those stories which are ghostly and romantic and which we term poetry.'

Both priests clearly agree.

'It is a yearning for the Holy Ghost, certainly,' says Chaplain Chaplin, and would continue, but Cerimonia is inexorable. 'And such stories will certainly spring up around the stones of an ancient cathedral like this one. Indeed, it is St Salt's Night tonight, when it is said – by the townspeople, of course – that the blessed souls in heaven make a trip to earth as though the glimmering stars walked the common ground. It is storied also in that hearthlight of the commonalty that by the intercession of that same St Salt all souls will gather in the cathedral clothed in bodies of light shaped in human form indeed but more exquisitely spiritual, and any who see them there will gain a little tinge of salvation that may overspread their souls entirely if they have intercourse with more than three of these souls. Yet such may also be damned utterly if seeing this sight they were to refuse this sacrament, for it is not sin but salvation, as on St Salt's Night salvation and sin move very close together; if indeed they were able to resist the fluence of the glorious perfumes and exquisite rustlings and whistlings every movement of these blessed creatures causes. It's a fine story, is it not?'

'An allegory of probable pagan origin . . .' Cerimonia is confident that both his listeners would have been more leisurely sceptical over the port and cigars, but recently teetotal and tobaccoless minds are very eager to be up and testing the world. 'But if you encountered such a manifestation, would you not wish to change tack and write another book, besides being damned if you refused participation?'

The archbishop takes a quick look at Chaplin before replying. 'There is no doubt of it. But if me no ifs. Without such a glory perceptible to the inner conscience and outer senses there would be no cause to change our stern doctrine. I am the Head of the Church, and it is for me to speak of what I know best, which is prayer and devotion. Glories such as you intimate are the reward of discipline.'

'Yet if the time came for such a manifestation on earth . . .'

Chaplin puts his nervous oar in. 'Then heaven and earth, blessing and sin, would, as you say, draw together, and the last judgment would be nigh. We can only watch and pray.'

'Tonight is St Salt's Night.' Cerimonia's voice drops a tone.

'If there were any truth to the tale, it would be easy to see from this palace.' The archbishop gets up restlessly and draws the curtain. 'But, as you see, the night is as black as the suggestion of your story.'

Cerimonia darts a finger forward. 'What are those crawling lights moving across the close?'

The archbishop leans forward. 'Merely reflections of the stars above in some rainwater.'

'The lights are scuttling across to the cathedral. It is like a procession of souls. There must be a thousand of them.'

'Open the window.'

The Master-thief

'There is a strange tapping and rustling.'

'It is something like a river of light lapping within the cloisters.'

'The cathedral great bell is beginning to sound.' Its tones are in the air, and its buzz underfoot.

'Lights have gone up in the chancel.' The archbishop lifts his empty hand to his mouth as if to pull on a lighted cigar.

'Stay behind me, My Lord. This is at the very least burglary.' Chaplin unbolts the front door.

The great cathedral's windows are ablaze with light. Cerimonia permits himself a grin and hurries into the close after the two priests. The Great West door of the cathedral opens slowly of its own accord.

'Oh, the blaze of light, the perfume, the rustling of colours, the banquet of smells!'

The archbishop and his staunch friend totter forward into the arms of the chorus of whores in their new dresses, who are singing sweeter than the cathedral adolescents ever did or could:

> *It is but a notion,*
> *The rumour of corruption,*
> *Earth's incapacity*
> *Here finds redress*
> *And ineffability*
> *Incarnates in love;*
> *Eternal womanhood*
> *Leads us above.*

> *For who unmanningly haunts the mountain ravened eaves*
> *Or skulks in the dell moon but moonshine echoing clear*
> > *From the starred well?*
> *A hill touches an angel. Out of a saint's cell*
> *The nightbird lauds through nunneries and domes of leaves*

> *Her robin breasted tree, three Marys in the rays.*
> Sanctum sanctorum *the animal eye of the wood*
> *In the rain telling its beads, and the gravest ghost*
> *The owl at its knelling. Fox and holt kneel before blood.*
> > *Now the tales praise*
> *The star rise at pasture and nightlong the fables graze*
> *On the lord's-table of the bowing grass.*

79

The master-thief leans over Bast's desk and explains his strategies once again. 'The archbishop is now perfectly well aware that the souls perambulating in the dark were five hundred crabs with lighted candles stuck in their own wax on the shells, and that the blessed souls in the cathedral who rose to their feet as the archbishop entered in his too-sober mufti, themselves clothed in the rainbow colours of the celestial regions rustling and whistling with the silk of it, were five hundred whores; nevertheless the heavens opened for him and his chaplain, and they were lost once they in-breathed a few molecules of the perfume exhaled by those ladies so taken with their new dresses and very anxious to please. So the archbishop and his chaplain were stolen from their church and saved into the bargain.'

'Indeed, saved many times over,' says Bast. He is grim but resigned. 'Master-thief, you have come into my domain and you have overturned it. During the execution of your three tasks you have undermined the discipline of my army and my confidence in it and its commanders; you have shown up my wife as over-credulous and undiscerning and myself as a miserable coward; and you have converted the religious leaders of the community to a pagan *horasis*, spiritual experience by sexual intercourse, a gnostic position. Now, by my own laws, you are to take your sister away and marry her, thus breaking one of the greatest prohibitions known to mankind, brother–sister marriage.'

'Let me see her. Is she still sleeping? My final task should be to awaken her.'

'She is in this secret bedchamber.' Bast touches a spring and panels slide open.

'May I kiss her?' The master-thief drops on his knees by the bed.

'You have earned the right. She is yours.'

'Mine for ever, as it was in the beginning. I have a message for her.'

He begins to speak.

> *Only for the turning of the earth in her holy*
> *Heart! Slyly, slowly, hearing the wound in her side go*
> *Round the sun, he comes to my love like the designed snow,*
> > *And truly he*
> *Flows to the strand of flowers like the dew's ruly sea,*
> *And surely he sails like the ship shape clouds. Oh he*

The Master-thief

Comes designed to my love to steal not her tide raking
Wound, nor her riding high, nor her eyes, nor kindled hair,
But her faith that each vast night and the saga of prayer
                                        He comes to take
Her faith that this last night for his unsacred sake
He comes to leave her in the lawless sun awaking

Naked and forsaken to grieve he will not come.
Ever and ever by all your vows believe and fear
My dear this night he comes and night without end my dear
                                Since you were born:
And you shall wake, from country sleep, this dawn and each first
    dawn,
Your faith as deathless as the outcry of the ruled sun.

His words cast their spell. The eyelids of the woman on the bed flutter
open.

'I dreamed that my brother kissed me, and left,' she says.

Count Bast looks around him, and turns to the colonel. 'Where is
the master-thief?'

'He has gone, My Lord.'

'He has stolen my heart,' says the master-thief's sister.

The Three Feathers

The Three Feathers

The king's sons stood around in the marble lobby of the palace chapel, waiting for the service to finish. Two of them were big fat beefy men with fair hair; the third you'd mistake for some kind of under-butler or house-scullion, quick, dark, retiring, shorter than the others. The two blond-moustached men were Grimald, the elder brother, and Rudolph, the middle one: they might have been twins; they were indistinguishable. The little Celtish man was usually known as Dummling, because he didn't speak much, though his given name was Dominic. The big hulkers were their father's sons all right; Dummling, latest from the womb, resembled his dead mother.

A roll of organ-music and the wail of priests came through the doors. The archbishop's voice began a sobbing song in a high tenor.

'They have nearly finished in there,' remarked Grimald.

'God will tell the king which of us shall be king,' said Rudolph.

'That screeching is the archbishop's peroration. God by now has told the king.'

Dummling said nothing, just leant against the wall with his hands in his pockets. The two identical brothers walked up and down. They were wearing heavy gold chains and tightly buttoned-up tunics, and spurs. Their hands were heavy with jewelled rings, which sparkled. Dummling wore soft dark leather and a white shirt, deeply open. The confident blond men talked about their inheritance in drawling voices.

They felt murderous about each other and about Dummling, but, until they knew which way the inheritance would be divided, they felt that the only certain thing was the old king's death.

'He doesn't frighten any more. You must be able to *terrify*,' said one of the big men.

'Are you frightened of our father, Dummling?' pausing in their stroll.

'Yes . . . No.'

'Come now,' said Grimald condescendingly, 'that is a very strange reaction. Yes and no. Inconceivable.'

'No,' said Rudolph, 'I can see what he means. I am not frightened of the king. I am frightened for him. He is old, and wears a heavy gold crown, and his neck is skinny. I am afraid it will snap his head off.'

'That would be terrible,' said Grimald, 'especially if it happened before he had chosen one of us.'

A conclusive roll of organ came through the door.

'Well, God has decided. It won't be long.'

'I was more frightened of Mother!' said Dummling.

'Frightened of Mother!' The other two were incredulous. 'Mother was a woman!'

'She had more power than we knew what to do with. So she died.'

'Mother? Power? The king has power. Not the queen. She may have had power over you, Dummling, but then you never did grow up properly, did you?' said Grimald, or it may have been Rudolph.

'The queen used to choose the kings.'

'Well, that is utter nonsense.'

'She would hold the great figured bowl with all the animals on it, the one that is in the museum, and the king would let her slit his arteries, and he would die on his knees while she took the blood from him.'

'Those times are over, thank God.'

'And she would cast the blood into the reservoir of drinking water and runners would take little pieces of the king's flesh that she cut off to be buried in the fields. The new king was the man who could watch this fate unafraid. She could smell fear, and death, and joy, and knew how to scent them out to cause more fear, more death or more joy.'

'Absolutely barbarous.'

'Better than men shut away in armour from each other sweating

86

fear and death. "Killing is a serious matter," Mother used to say, "and best left to the queen and king."'

'It is a great pleasure to kill,' remarked Grimald thoughtfully, 'especially with the big two-handed sword. If you get it swinging right, it is like a bacon-slicer. I once got the teenage grand-duke like that, on an upwards stroke, where his legs forked. I shall never forget the look on his face, as much as I could see of it through his visor, as he watched his tripes fall out of him. I remember I tore my helmet and my habergeon off and rubbed him all over my hair and face and across my chest. He smelt like warm seaweed, but I got a charge from doing this like a bolt of lightning.'

'In the queen's day, it was the electricity of the king only that went into the ground. There was no waste like that. The riches inside him were everybody's.'

'Yes, yes, I've heard your opinions about that sort of thing before, Dummling, and I can only say that I don't mind if we meet in battle, since I'd enjoy it if you wouldn't.'

'Yes, Dummling, we all know you're a mother's boy. God decides now. He is king of kings, king squared, and the king is Head of Church and State. Unfortunately our father is almost worn out.'

'And we are almost new, eh Rudolph?'

The big oak doors of the chapel banged wide and out strode a tall, moustached blond man the same size and appearance as Rudolph and Grimald, but dressed in blazing silver armour like a set of mirrors. As he clanked towards them the virile sounds of his accoutrements were almost deafening. They came from an acolyte trotting behind him who had a complicated apparatus of tambourines and speaking-horns. This was the Virile-Noise Maker whose function was to see that the king made the sounds appropriate to his station: such as Grimald and Rudolph could make in their young manhood, festooned with ornamental chains and, at times, armour, and which Dummling did not care to make in his soft noiseless clothes.

It was important that the king gave off all the panoply of signs and sound of kingship, and it was the custom that he should do so up to the point of his death. The king usually died standing up in armour, or sitting on the great 'rainbow throne', which was wheeled out of its shrine when it was decided that the monarch was *in extremis*. The armour in which the kings died was a complex frame on castors with an apparatus of cogs that worked the legs in phoney-vigorous strides.

The moribund king would be clipped into this and wheeled about. The rainbow throne was an epiphany, and much preferred for death. It was constructed so as to appear continually in motion, and to give off a soft whispering sound, like the wind in trees, and to break the ordinary light from the palace windows up into rainbows. The effect was as if the king were sitting within a lightly sounding waterfall that refracted the light into myriad colours. This happened by means of diamonds and gems of every hue set among spun gold and silver threads, all the parts reflecting and refracting each other, and kept in continual motion by means of a crank operated by the Virile-Noise Maker. As the king sat on his throne *in articulo mortis* a functionary held his dagger at the throat of this behind-the-scenes acolyte. At the moment of the king's death, the dagger plunged, and the rainbow throne fell silent and still. A solemn voice called out, 'The king is dead.' The seated corpse then disappeared, with the aid of a confusing apparatus of mirrors and trapdoors seeming to melt into the throne. As the seat fell vacant, the assembled crowd of nobles would shout, 'Long live the king!' and the new king would stride forward, his own Virile-Noise Maker following, and take his place on the rainbow throne, which would begin its rustling dance again, the replacement acolyte having taken his place at the crank.

The big blond king strode forward from the chapel, noisily, and all the people watching knew that the blond locks were a wig, the moustache dyed, and the beautiful armour of mirrors mere Bacofoil which soon would be too creased to wear much longer, and would have to be replaced. Close up, the lips were slack and the blue eyes rheumy. Grimald and Rudolph stood to attention, and eyed the king with a proprietorial air. Dummling respectfully took his hands out of his pockets.

'God cannot decide,' said the old king.

'God knows everything, sire,' replied Grimald. Rudolph kept his peace, though his chains clanked and his spurs rattled.

'Then he's not telling,' said the king impatiently. 'The archbishop says I must take the oracle.'

This was surprising, since oracles were against the law in this kingdom. Everybody used them, but they were against the law. The penalties for attempting to import oracles were as severe as those laid down for people smuggling pets. Rabies and oracles were feared equally as a kind of madness. It was the custom here to calculate ceremonial effects, and not leave them to chance.

'Send to China for an I Ching,' offered Rudolph.

'To Spain for a Tarot pack,' drawled Grimald.

'Let's do it here,' said Dummling.

His brothers looked at him as though he had suggested that there was hydrophobia in the soil. The old king smiled at Dummling, and signalled with his hand. Chairs were slid forwards, and they all sat down, except Dummling.

'No, not here, Father. Let's go outside,' he said.

Lackeys opened doors and carried chairs. At length the three sons and the father were sitting under a sky that promised rain, in a courtyard that had been left unpaved. Palace revisionists, those for instance who had built on the marble hall and the chapel they had just left, had never been able to break with tradition sufficiently to get this centre courtyard properly guttered and flagged with dressed stone, though everybody agreed it was an eyesore, and very unhygienic, a quag when it rained hard, and a dustbowl in summer. The offering of flowers was made each June on the wooden steps in the north by a representative of each of the provinces. This was a very old custom, politically unsound to change. The people had grumbled enough that a priest received the flowers nowadays, since the priestesses had gone. They handled this by getting the most feminine of the bishops to grow his hair and wear rouge. None of the people was taken in, but the form was right.

'Here?' said Grimald to his father. 'This is just an earthen court-yard.'

'The succession should be decided in the Golden Hall!' The two elder brothers were not going to be left out of this. If the old king in his dotage wanted oracles, then they knew oracles.

'By aeromancy,' exclaimed Rudolph.

'Divination by cloud-shapes contemplated as we lie on our backs on great brocade mattresses, the archbishop pointing out the pictures in the air with his long wand.'

'By capnomancy,' said Rudolph. Would his brother know this one? He did.

'We cast greasy powders into the hearth big as a church porch and we watch the eloquence of the coloured smokes.' The brothers were stolid, but, like every member of an educated court, capable of flights of fancy. Dummling held his peace. This suited his peacock brothers.

'By cromniomancy.'

'The king lifts the lid of the great warm tureen incubated in a remote cellar, and by the light of the lamp full of snake oil we study the shapes of the onion-sprouts. They all lean in one direction. They could point at you, Dummling!'

'He's the only onion-king, the turnip!' said Grimald.

'Scarecrow-king, more likely,' sneered Rudolph.

'King of the blackbirds,' muttered Dummling. There was a pause.

'Hippomancy.'

'We choose the king by the stamping of the horses in the royal cellars.'

'Phyllorhodomancy.'

'The royal gardener takes the sacred rose and hands it obsequiously to the king who slaps its crimson petals against the palm of his hand and the sounds of this speak his successor's name.'

'Pantisocromancy.'

'Every dish in the kitchens, every fly in the bedrooms, every leaf in the gardens, speaks equally the name of the new king.'

'Except that they don't,' said the king.

'No, sire, they don't,' agreed Rudolph quickly.

Then Dummling broke in.

'We can do it here. Without stirring a foot. There will be something to tell us here, in the plain earth.' He looked around and picked up three long white feathers that were lying by a red stone. The two brothers turned again towards the king, trying to divert him from such nonsense.

'Archepiscomancy!'

'Divination by cutting off the archbishop's head.'

'Decimatomancy!'

'Divination by killing one in ten.'

'Praefectus-praetoriomancy!'

'Divination by killing the general of the armies.'

'Massacromancy!'

'Divination by killing everybody.'

When the brothers had finished riddling, Dummling spoke again.

'We can decide this now, if you want. Father, take these three feathers in your hand. Now, think what you would most like your son the king to bring to show he is fit to govern the realm.'

'Dominic,' said the old king faintly, 'I think I want a – carpet.'

It was the turn of the two elder brothers to mutter under their breath.

'A carpet! Oh, *Father*.' That was the middle son.

'I want a kingdom. I shall be pleased to give him one for a carpet. Six foot long with daisies on it, preferable,' said Grimald.

'We used to have a most beautiful carpet in the throne-room,' said the king. 'All the people who came to ask me boons would have to walk the length of this carpet, as it was laid like a path to the throne. I really think I gave wiser answers for the pondering of that carpet. Its pattern was – abstract – but I could see many things in it as I considered my suppliants' problems: a gazelle, a galleon, a banquet, a knot-garden, the queen's shape as she seemed to advance towards me along the pattern, turn and retreat, having been dead many a year, poor dear. I soon realised that the images gave me answers, and my advice became famous. But so many people came that the carpet wore out. The son that brings a kingly carpet like this will be the ruler.'

'Father,' said Dummling, 'raise your hand with the feathers in it to your lips and say, "You shall go as the feather goes," and blow them out into the air. We'll each of us look for a carpet in the direction where our feather falls.'

The king puffed at the feathers, and they rose up in the air and spiralled round. Grimald's fell to the east, and he was pleased about this, since he knew that the best carpets came from the Orient. Rudolph's slid to the west, and he was pleased too, as he knew that it was only in the west that people could afford to have good carpets.

Dummling's feather spiralled highest in the air, but it fell straight down and lay just by the king's feet, not one inch had it moved in either direction.

'Ah,' said Grimald, 'the feather that didn't go anywhere. You could get the old carpet out of the box-room, Dummling, and give it a scrub. It might do. Or you could draw one on the floor, couldn't you?'

'Hello, Brother Grimald. Where's your carpet?'

Grimald pulled a stained white silk cloth out of his inner pocket, and winked. Silk was nice to wipe oneself with, and enjoyed a reputation as an impenetrable contraceptive.

'To tell you the truth I couldn't be bothered. I rode east and I came to that inn I always wanted to visit, and I stopped for a glass of cider, and I saw these girls . . . and, well, you know, my bags were full of money. I've never felt so relaxed in my life. What about yourself? I don't see anything . . .'

Rudolph pulled a black silk cloth out of his wallet, and winked. It was stained also. The stains were white.

'Oh, I had a use for a silk handkerchief also, Grimald. I feel totally better for the holiday. Do you know, I think we should join forces. It doesn't much matter which of us rules, so long as we get equal shares. There was never any risk of Dummling begging, borrowing or stealing a carpet of any kingliness at home, where his oath bound him to stay, so why should I bother? Or you? The king's quite loopy; these whims fly in and out of his head like the feathers themselves.'

'We ought to nobble Dummling. Could we lend him one of these hankies and give him a disease? He was always delicate.'

'It's simple. We'll indict him immediately for bringing back the old magic. Where is he anyway?'

'I was told to report to the throne room.'

They spoke in whispers now, as two halberdiers were marching along the corridor to escort them to the king. The brothers' spirits lifted even higher as they realised that they were being taken to the room of the rainbow throne. It must mean that the king was in a poor way. They heard the soughing of the throne through the double-doors, but when these were thrown open they were dazzled not only by the expected magnificence of the rainbow throne but of the king too, seated upright on it in full regalia, looking twice the man he was when they left. Starting from their feet a magnificent carpet like a garden in full bloom stretched to his footstool. The king watched them, and they knew he could see their evil hearts in the pattern of the carpet. They advanced humbly, and kissed their father's hand, and he smiled as if all were forgiven. They knew that the carpet had given him the strength to rule a little longer, and that Dummling would have the kingdom when he grew feeble again.

'Dummling! We want a word with you.'

'Where did you get that bloody great carpet?'

'Look, chaps, you're not going to believe this, but . . .'

'You're going to tell us anyway.'

'Only if you want.'

'Look, we just don't believe that carpet grew . . .'

'Very well,' said Dummling. He seemed to have grown smaller and darker since they had been away, and more tense. He had a little dry cough. The brothers loomed over him, and he looked away and around, dartingly, as though there might be listeners. He gestured to them to come out into the courtyard, and, when they clanked out over the dry earth, he stopped them with a hand gently laid on Grimald's shoulder, and motioned to them to take off their spurs. With a look at each other, they did so. Their understanding was that Dummling had been practising some kind of the old magic, and was therefore likely to be on the edge of insanity. If that was so, they might as well listen and encourage his illness, then he would be no further problem to them.

'You remember that my feather went nowhere, but just fell down and stayed where it was? Well of course I was pretty fed up by this. You just went off, Grimald to the east and Rudolph to the west, and I couldn't think what to do to help the old king. I was nearly crying because he looked so feeble under that awful armour, and all his talk about carpets. I began to scuff the ground with my foot, and I noticed something under the top layer of dirt. It was the planks of a trapdoor, with a lifting-ring set in it. There was nothing better to do, so I grasped the ring, and twisted it, and the trapdoor opened. There was a flight of stone steps going down into the ground.'

'Pull the other one, it's got feathers on it,' said Rudolph, with hostility. Grimald laid his hand on his arm, as if to remind him of their alliance. 'No, please, dear brother, finish your tale. It's a very remarkable one.'

'At the bottom of these stairs was a short corridor and a light shining. There was a closed door with a crescent shape cut in it high up, and the eerie blue-green light came from this. I rattled the latch, but it was locked. So I stood still, doing nothing.'

Now the brothers were quite convinced that Dummling had gone crazy, because he started limping in a circle round the courtyard with a kind of dragging step with a little hop in it every now and again. He turned on them suddenly and, with his eyes blazing called out, 'IT IS HERE. IT IS NOW,' pointing at the ordinary earth at his feet. The brothers expected to see a trapdoor, but there was nothing. Then Dummling resumed his little dance, speaking softly. The brothers craned to listen.

'Then I heard a little high soprano voice singing inside . . .' and Dummling sang, and it was as though another person had got into his face:

> '*Virgin, green and small,*
> *Oh, little shrivel-leg,*
> *Point the bone, point the bone,*
> *Shrivel to and fro;*
> *Let's see who comes down to us.*

'The door very, very slowly, like a planet sliding on its orbit, opened inwards.

'There was a cavern behind the door. I could see the roots of immense trees like rafters, and colossal blocks of masonry clearly older than our palace. The stone under my feet was polished like a mirror, and spread out in front of me like a dark ballroom floor. In the middle was what I thought was a great boulder which licked its lips and then I saw it was a toad. I looked past the spreading snout of smile and the eyes big as footballs opened. They were as blue as a summer sky. The front claws were planted on the stone like warted roots, foot to foot with the massive reflection, and, as I looked down past it, I seemed to see clouds drift past in an under-sky. Round the great toad were twelve small boulders.'

'This is a fantasy!' whispered Grimald to Rudolph. 'Listen to him. I suspect our dear little brother is shamanising, and that's forbidden too.'

'As I watched, all twelve boulders opened their eyes blue as the summer sky and it was as bright as day under the ground. The big toad opened its mouth and I knew the tongue could lash out like a leather belt and roll me up in stickiness. Instead it spoke to me.'

The sky seemed to grow darker as little Dummling hopped round his circle speaking with his own voice and with another's that was deep and rich as a tun of Guinness. It reminded Grimald of the madam at the Cathouse Inn, a famous black who was reputed to stand in her clients' bedrooms watching them fuck, invisible in the darkness. It was said that this served them right for fucking with the light out.

'I see you have made your way safely down here, Dummling,' said Dummling. 'Now tell me what you want with us. You must lack something. Something you want brought you here.'

'Ma'am,' said Dummling, in his own voice, clearing his throat as a frightened person might, 'Ma'am . . . ?'

'Ma'am will do nicely,' said the other voice.

'Ma'am, I need a kingly carpet.'

'Do you, indeed? Is it for yourself?'

'For my father, ma'am. My father the king.'

'Why did he not come himself?'

'He is close to death, ma'am.'

'That would have made his descent all the easier.'

'He wanted a carpet, by whose pattern one of his sons could rule, brought into the kingdom.'

'And that son is you?'

'I claim nothing for myself, ma'am. I am doing as my father wished, and as the feather showed me. Besides, I do not think they'd let me rule after . . .'

'Well?'

'After talking to you, ma'am.'

'Virgin, green and small, Oh, little shrivel-leg, Oh, little withershins bring me the tree,' said the dark voice.

'Oh that carpet!' Dummling cried out. 'The small toads drag the great tree in, one half brilliant green and the other half blazing red, and you take the bark in your claw and with a quick flip unroll the tree into a carpet. If I sat deep in the earth for ever, I could hardly follow out all those patterns.'

'You'll get your chance to sit in the earth and watch the patterns,' replied Dummling's dark voice. 'Meanwhile, take this carpet to your father. It won't mean as much up there as it does down here, but it will mean something, and that's not nothing.'

'I thank you humbly, ma'am.'

Black laughter poured out of Dummling's mouth.

'Oh, we're all 'umble down 'ere, you know, 'umble as 'umans ought to be, Dummling, 'umble as 'umus.'

The laughter stopped abruptly. Dummling closed his mouth with a snap and stood looking at his brothers. Rudolph avoided his gaze. Grimald strolled over to where Dummling was standing, and scuffed the earth with his beautifully polished hunting-boot. Dummling coughed painfully.

'I see no trapdoor.'

'It's not there when you look for it, Grimald.'

The chapel doors banged back on the marble walls, and the king strode out.

'A ring! A ring! The one who brings me a kingly ring will be my heir.'

'Here we go again,' said Grimald.

'Dummling, bring me the feathers,' ordered the king.

'Dummling,' said Grimald, 'I thought the king had given you the kingdom.'

'Yes. But he seemed so much better I gave it him back again,' said Dummling, opening the wooden box in which the feathers were kept.

'Well, that didn't last, did it?' hissed Grimald after his retreating back.

'You shall go as they fly. You shall go as the feathers blow,' said the king, his feeble puff assisted by the Virile-Noise Maker, who had a large fan.

Grimald's big red face turning grinning to Dummling. 'Well, yours got nowhere again, little Dummling. I'm off to the east, where they dig kingly rings out of the ground.'

'And I'm off to the west, where the shops are full of them. Goodbye, Your Majesty!'

'Good riddance,' said the king, *sotto voce*.

Time passed, and the brothers found themselves interviewing Dummling in the earthen courtyard again. He lived there, now, and had put up a tent of skins. The damp air had made his cough worse. The big blond brothers had come back, empty-handed as usual, full of post-coital contentment, reminiscing about the maps of Ireland on their handkerchiefs. Again they were summoned to the rainbow throne room, and again they found a renewed king. They were compelled humbly to kiss his gold and diamond ring, which he said talked to him in his sleep, and in which they felt he could see their evil hearts.

'I suppose you got the ring by going nowhere and doing nothing, again.'

'Well, I do nothing in my way, and you do nothing in yours,' said Dummling.

'Tell us.'

'I'd rather not.'

'We insist.'

Dummling went into his shambling dance, to and fro over the small space in the courtyard.

'I stared at that white feather settled on the dirt floor a long time. I was angry with you, and envious too, for setting out so cheerfully on your nonsense. But then my anger disappeared, and I started laughing at all the things you'd get up to, behind your silk handkerchiefs. Then when I finished laughing I found I was looking down into the dirt and I saw that the trapdoor was there again, but it was ajar this time. I squirmed through the hole, and went down the little stairs which were much brighter because the crescent cut in the door was almost full, and I rattled at the latch.'

The high voice sang from his lips again:

'Virgin, green and small,
Oh, little shrivel-leg,
Oh, little withershins,
Point the bone, point the bone,
Shrivel to and fro.'

His own voice continued.

'As soon as the song began the door opened easily and I was in the cavern with its dark floor and its roof of tightly woven roots. The great toad was there looking like a rock and she opened her eyes and her attendant boulders opened their eyes and the room was as bright as noon.'

'It was easier to get down this time, wasn't it, Dummling?' said the other black voice as Dummling hopped and limped. 'What is your need on this occasion? Something for yourself, or for your father?'

'My father, ma'am.'

'Then I'm not sure you should have it. You should ask me for something for yourself.'

'It is something I want myself. For my father.'

'They never learn. Very well. Tell me. Never mind. I know already. Virgin, green and small, Oh, little shrivel-leg, Oh, little withershins, bring me the TREE.'

'That great tree!' called out Dummling in his own voice, 'one half burning red, one half emerald-green, how the light pours out of it as you open the bark like a lid! The blaze turns your dark skin white: how can you bear to reach with your great claw into such radiation! It is like plucking the sun out of the ground . . .'

'It is easy for me, Dummling. I am used to the brightness inside things. Here is the ring. Put it on your finger.'

'I will take it to my father, and put it on his!'

And Dummling stopped speaking and stared at his brothers, who stared back.

'It won't last, Dummling,' said Rudolph. Dummling coughed miserably. One foot dragged all the time now.

The chapel doors banged back, and the Virile-Noise Maker raised a speaking-trumpet to the king's pale lips.

'Now I know!' he lisped through it. 'My sons, you must bring home your brides. I will give the kingdom to the most beautiful among my sons' brides!'

'Try my feathers, sire,' crooned Rudolph, offering a box of marked feathers. The king ignored him. Again Dummling's feather fell like lead.

'That does it, I think, Dummling,' said Grimald. 'You won't find a bride in this old place. Only dead women dwell here: our mother, the old priestesses. You can't marry dust, Dummling.'

Time passed. The brothers had returned, not empty-handed this time, but with brides. They had all been summoned to an audience in the rainbow throne room. The soughing that came through the doors was louder than before, and Grimald and Rudolph felt confident that death was near.

'I would like you to meet my bride-to-be, dark-haired Gretchen, who comes from a house just beyond the West Gate, brother,' said Rudolph, with flourishes.

'I know that house well. I'm honoured.'

'It's a greater honour for me,' said Gretchen.

'No, it's a greater honour for me. Allow me to present my fiancée, fair Matilda, from the inn quite near the East Gate.'

'Ah, the inn. Charmed, I'm sure.' Matilda said nothing. 'You certainly do like sturdy girls, Rudolph.'

'Well, Grimald, I always did. But what about the forearms on Matilda? Are you taking up wrestling, dear brother?'

'Do you really need such a bodyguard, yourself, Rudolph?' The brothers now wanted dynasties, and were feeling murderous again. They had quite forgotten Dummling, whom they knew could not have found a bride, being honour-bound not to travel outside the palace.

Yet, when they entered the throne room, they were dazzled by three rainbow thrones, and a lady with hair red as blood on the middle throne, wearing a golden crown, and Dummling and the king flanking her, also crowned. The brothers looked at their brides and saw nothing in their faces except the most profound social discomfort. Then Dummling began to speak in his many voices from the left-hand throne.

'When you left me to go your merry way, I thought of the kingdom in your spendthrift hands, and I sat down in despair and stared at the dirt where the white feather had fallen. I sank down and down into myself and my black thoughts – then I came to and realised that I was standing under the earth in the little corridor full of blue-green light in front of the latched door, and the green transom was no longer a half-globe but full and round. I touched the door lightly with a finger and it opened . . .'

The soprano song came from his full red lips:

> 'Virgin, green and small
> Oh, little shrivel-leg
> Point the bone, point the bone
> Dummling's underground again.'

'What now, Dummling?' came the black voice.

'The most beautiful woman in the world!'

'For yourself or your father, Dummling?'

'For myself, Madame Toad. Is she in the tree?'

'She was.'

'And the great toad scooped out with her claw and picked up one of the smaller toads that sat round her.'

'Here, Dummling, this is your bride. Lead her out of here with love and you will find that she looks different in the sunlight.'

'So I walked my toad out of the cavern and up through the corridor and the trapdoor, and I found myself helping this lady by her hand out into the sunlight – allow me to introduce my bride! Zoe, meet my two brothers by blood and my two new sisters.' Dummling got up and walked over without a limp to the middle throne.

Grimald ignored his outstretched hand and spoke angrily to the king.

'It was pre-judged. Dummling was crowned before the beauty of our brides was shown. You were sitting on the thrones before we even returned with our treasures.'

'My Liege, our father,' said Rudolph, more circumspectly, 'we demand another, final test. We demand that the three brides be tested.'

The king stared at his carpet, with his ring-finger in his ear.

'Hang up a barrel-hoop from the rafters,' he said, as his ring told him to. 'Let the three women leap through the hanging hoop. She who leaps best shall be queen, and her husband will rule the kingdom. This is the fourth and final test.'

'You can do that, Matilda,' said Grimald.

'Gretchen, your strong legs will leap that far easily,' said Rudolph.

Matilda got her bullet-head down and sprinted at the hoop, which, at a gesture from the king, the halberdiers had set swinging dangerously. Her timing was bad, and the heavy wood clouted her. She fell unconscious to the floor. Grimald ran to her and began chafing her wrists.

Gretchen cleared the rim of the hoop all right, and her timing was excellent, but she was short on power and came down inside the hoop, so that she hung ludicrously, swinging from the ceiling, like somebody wearing an enormous belt round their middle.

Now it was Zoe's turn. She put her crown aside and drew down her red brows on her cream-white forehead and hunched her shoulders, and suddenly looked extremely ugly. She crouched on the floor and the skirts of her dress looked like enormous webbed feet. It was strange how so beautiful a woman could look so animal. Then she launched herself into the air and cleared the hoop with great ease, seeming to hang in the air as she went through the very centre, descending in a gentle curve, and becoming herself again on the other side, shaking her hair out and laughing. Rudolph and Grimald, who were comforting their brides, looked at each other.

'It looks as though shamanism is here to stay,' said the eldest brother.

'You win, Dummling,' said Rudolph.

'We must ask the king who wins,' replied Dummling.

Then Zoe spoke to him. 'The king is dead, Your Majesty,' she said.

The Juniper Tree

The Juniper Tree

MOTHER SAYS: I will eat my apple in the open air
Under the snow-holding juniper. How spare the
   wind is,
Like a sharp juice spread on my skin;
Let me unpeel the apple with my silver knife.
Oh, a little cut. Now the blood-juice flows!
I shake my hand, thus, across the snow-bank.
The blood's piercing red sinks in the snow
Under the evergreen juniper! That is what I need,
As I need God, as I need green,
A child as red as blood and white as snow.
I feel it has already happened, I feel so happy.
And now a month passes, and the snow is gone,
Two months, and the earth greens,

And the birds hop in the perfumes of the trees,
The incense of their green; now the blossoms fall
Twisting down like a warm snow, and five months
   gone
Under the juniper tree it smells so sweet because
Its fruit is coming, and here I am

On my knees praying to the tree, how foolish,
And six months gone the fruit shines
In its needles, and over the steely berries
They call kill-bastard my hand hovers,
Wishing to pick come what may
And seven months gone I cram the juniper fruit
Into my mouth until the tart juice runs,
And my happiness is gone, they have made me ill,
And eight months gone I make my husband promise
'When I die,
Bury me under the juniper tree' and I
Am happy again for nine months gone
I bear my child white as the snow
And red as blood, and my happiness
Is so great I die.

NORMAN SAYS: And one month gone, I am so unhappy,
I never thought a man could cry so much
Under the juniper tree; and she's gone
A month and the nightly storms
Have tattered the juniper, and I tidy
The garden, and my tears flow
Under the juniper tree, its scent
Catches my throat, there is
Lightning and distant thunder, pillars of light
Like ladders to heaven clambering from fields
Of vividest sunshine, the larches
Thin and the beeches burn bare,
And under the dark green of the juniper tree
I remember her, she is bones
In the root-pattern, and the juniper needles
Perfume the quick sunbeams, and three months
   gone
The grass is frosty, except in the shade
Under the juniper tree, and the gate clicks
And I look up and see another woman
And walk out from the juniper shadow . . .

Here are my two children feasting
On apples for breakfast. Nine years have passed.
My grief makes me work, makes money.

Now I have a second wife,
A little daughter by her, and a son
So delicate, his skin white as snow,
His lips red as blood, just a year older.
She's a strapping lass, like her mother, is Anne-
Marie.

He's a bit thin, poor lad, Victor,
A bit of a weed, but he'll plump out.

STEPMOTHER EVE
SAYS:

Victor, I wish you'd eat up your porridge.
I won't give you apples if it spoils your appetite
For porridge; look at Anne-Marie here, she's
A year younger than you but twice as strong;
Do you want to be a weakling all your life?
Eat up your porridge. Clumsy boy,
Now you've knocked your plate into your lap,
Can't you do anything right, weed as you are?

NORMAN SAYS:

That's enough, Eve. It puts me off breakfast
The way you go on at the boy.

EVE SAYS:

I never met your first wife, Norman, but he must
take after her;
I don't want him mooning off and dying;
And I want that juniper tree chopped down;
It's getting too close to the window; it makes
The house damp and gives him a fever;
Look at his hectic cheeks, near blood-red;
Haven't you finished clearing up that mess yet?
You're always in the way, you don't help out
Like Anne-Marie does. Go and get yourself more
porridge.

NORMAN SAYS:

There isn't time. I must take him to school now
Or I'll be late for work.

EVE SAYS:

That's right
Take him off. Anne-Marie will stay
And help Mummy in the house all day
Until the pest returns.

NORMAN SAYS:

Eve! I wish you'd be just a bit kinder.

EVE SAYS: I will when he's a better boy. Give us a kiss then.
Ugh. You're all sticky with milk.

*

STEPDAUGHTER
ANNE-MARIE
SAYS: Mother, can I have an apple from the chest?
The lid's too heavy for me to lift.

EVE SAYS: Yes, of course you can, my dear.
Never try to help yourself. You see,
The lid is heavy and the edge is sharp.
You might easily cut your fingers off.

ANNE-MARIE
SAYS: Thank you, Mummy. Victor will be back
From school soon. Shall I get one for him too?
Whatever's the matter, Mother!
You frown
As though the Devil was looking at you.

EVE SAYS: What? No you can't. And I'll have back
The apple you've got. It's not time for tea.
Why should you have fruit before your brother!
Anyway I disapprove of snacks between meals.

ANNE-MARIE
SAYS: But . . .

EVE SAYS: I'm shutting the lid.

ANNE-MARIE
SAYS: But here he is, Mummy, coming up the path.

EVE SAYS: Anne-Marie! Go upstairs and tidy your hair.
Before your father comes back . . .
Would you like an apple, son?

VICTOR SAYS: Yes please, Stepmummy.

EVE SAYS: I wish you'd call me Mummy
Or my name, Eve.
Give us a kiss then.

VICTOR SAYS: Mummy, you look so terrible.

EVE SAYS: What do you mean! Always complaining. Give us
    a kiss.
Or would you rather have your apple?

All right then. I'll hold the lid for you.
Pick your own from the chest.
Lean in – now – I slam the sharp edge shut!
There you are, my boy! Your head
Rolls among the red apples, kissing them red.

ANNE-MARIE SAYS
(FROM UPSTAIRS):   Mummy . . .

EVE SAYS: Mummy . . . a mother . . . how could a
     mother . . . ?
What have I done! I shall be hanged.
Norman will turn against me
I shall lose my pretty home
The men will come and drag me to prison.
Can I make him as guilty somehow?
Can I implicate him? Or her?

ANNE-MARIE
SAYS: Mummy?

EVE SAYS: Or her. Yes, make it our female secret
And bind my own daughter.
Where is that white cloth
I ironed yesterday? I'll prop the corpse
And Victor shall sit up in this wooden chair.
Quick, a bowl of warm water. I can get the head
Out of the chest and sponge it clean
And wipe the neck and set the head on it
And bind it firmly with the white cloth
And set the chair against the light
In the kitchen doorway, and put an apple
In his hand. Now I'll stand by the range
Where the big pot of water is heating up,
Stirring it, round and round,
Round and round.

ANNE-MARIE
SAYS: Mummy? Mummy, Victor's sitting outside.
He has an apple in his hand and looks so ill.
I asked him for the apple but he wouldn't answer.

EVE SAYS: Ask him again, and if he won't answer
Box his ears for him. Just a bit.

ANNE-MARIE
SAYS:

Oh Mummy, I tried to kiss him and his head . . .
Oh, it was terrible how his head
Like meat fell from his shoulders.

EVE SAYS:

What, what have you done? They'll hang you
For this, my child. We must keep it secret,
A sacred secret, to keep you alive,
A holy secret we'll act out together.
In the old days, child,
In the holy days, the fairy days,
The days of the tales, the ancient days,
They'd kill a child in a holy way.

ANNE-MARIE
SAYS:

Oh

EVE SAYS:

Yes in a holy way, they'd kill a child
And eat him because he was so young
And tender like a lamb, and he was holy
Because his spirit would go on to God,
Because he was young and beautiful,
And plead with God because he was innocent,
So it was a holy thing . . .

ANNE-MARIE
SAYS:

Poor Victor

EVE SAYS:

A holy thing. Never girls,
Only the boys knew their way to God,
It is a terrible thing to be a woman
Without access to God, but we have the boys
Like carrier pigeons to angel our messages
And plead for us . . .

ANNE-MARIE
SAYS:

– A terrible thing to be a woman?

EVE SAYS:

Yes, my dear, I haven't told you yet,
You always get blamed for everything,
If there's anything wrong, you'll carry the can.
Victor will render into a delicious broth.
There now, don't cry, it's a holy thing,
Or cry your woman's tears into the pot
To salt it as I stir . . . Make wish as I stir,

Make a woman's wish as you eat . . .
This is the only way
A woman can find her path to God –
With a holy play, a holy cruel play . . .

*

NORMAN SAYS: – I could eat a horse. Where's Victor?
This stew is good. Where is my son?
I want to ask him about his lessons
It's not so important for a girl
But a boy must be good at his lessons
If he's to keep his wife and family,
It's a burden lightened by good schooling.
A woman must bear, and son learn. Where's Victor?

EVE SAYS: Oh, he went to his mother's great-uncle.
I said he could stay there.
He never said goodbye to me.
It's his nature. I said
He could stay six weeks.
Great-uncle's a classics scholar;
The stay will be good for him.

NORMAN SAYS: This is a really good scouse.
Have you got any more? It's so good
I'm surprised I feel sad at Victor going
Without saying goodbye. What an exquisite
Flavour. And, Anne-Marie,
Why are you crying?
I felt sad too, but,
Here, look, food's the answer to that;
Eve, heap up her plate. Oh,
Here's a little bone of the lamb that made
This fine scouse. What a shame,
A little square bone, poor thing,
But the tender meat tastes so good.

EVE WHISPERS: I got a little finger
With the nail still on it.
We're lost if he finds one.

NORMAN SAYS: Get me a dish for the bones, Eve,
You'll not want me to throw them

109

Under the table.
Oh, that was good. I think I'll just have a nap.

ANNE-MARIE Oh, poor Victor, you're more a part of us now
SAYS: Than you ever were, I can't stop crying.
How can I give my brother a proper funeral in public
Without burying my father, my mother and myself,
As we deserve, we all deserve, after that feast?
I can funeral his bones here and now,
The fingerbones like plum-stones round Father's
    plate,
And I can sieve what's left of the stew
To save the saucer-bones of his skull
That have sunk to the bottom,
And I can wash them and dry them all
And lay them in my red and green silk scarf
(What a small pile they make!)
And I can wrap them in the shining silk
And carry them out (my tears feel sticky and hot
Like tears of blood) to the juniper tree.
I remember there is a hole in its roots
Just the size for his bones in their silk bag
Where the green grass springs out in a tuft
And how brisk the wind is today as I drop them in,
It is in the juniper, and its boughs
Seem to open out and shut again
Like the hands of someone
Who is really happy, and there is a mist
Running out of the tree and it has
A bright centre like the sun, no,
There's a bird flying out of the mist,
Crying so sweetly like the whole of summer,
I can't quite see it, but there's red and green
And plumage that scatters light like white fire.
There! It's gone. The mist's gone.
Are his bones safe in the tree?
I think they've gone; they must have
Slid in deeper, out of sight, in their silk bag deep
Underground, where they belong. But
I feel so happy, as if he had never died.

The Juniper Tree

THE BIRD SINGS:

Butchered by Stepmother,
Devoured by Father,
Gathered up by half-sister
Anne-Marie –
She wrapped up the bones of me
In silk, in fine silk
And laid them inside the juniper tree.
I am become a great bird accordingly,
Reborn of my true mother's tree
In plumage like fire! Like blood!
Like gold! Like wildfire!
Like leaves! Like gold!

THE METALSMITH
SOLILOQUISES:

I haven't been a metalsmith all these years
Without knowing a singing bird when I see one.
It is the drab birds that sing most exquisitely.
The dung-coloured dusty birds – and the plumage,
Well, song is spent on plumage, it's one or the
    other.
For instance, parrots gaudy as flying blooms
Of the jungle blare like tuning wireless
Or croak in human transistor a garden or two
    away,
Quack quack, and 'pretty polly' and 'how's your
    uncle' then;
Rubbish. So when a bird looking like this one,
With the head of a hawk and the colours of a parrot,
Bronze and gold with a sheen of tin and silver,
The colours of all the metals I work in,
Comes flying like flaming banners,
I know it cannot sing.
If I make a singing bird,
As I have for all the crowned heads of the continent,
It has to have cogs of wood to sing –
Gold feathers cannot sing.

He's just a looker, this one,
I know a melodious bird when I see one.
It is not like a flying piece of rainbow,
It does not carry its fine head like a human child,
It does not have pinions splashed with eyes.

Sitting on my fence by the workshop in the early
    sun,
As I work on my masterpiece, this gold chain
May give me visual inspiration
But it cannot sing, it clanks.

THE BIRD SINGS:

Butchered by Stepmother,
By Father devoured,
Gathered in half-sister's
Fine silk scarf,
She picked up the bones of me,
Did Anne-Marie,
In silk, in fine silk
And laid them in the juniper tree.
I am become a great bird accordingly
In plumage like fire! Like gold!
Like blood! Like leaf!
Reborn from my mother's tree.

THE METALSMITH
SAYS:

Oh what a song! It made the gold brighter,
The gold I do not own that I work so hard in.
How can I make it sing again?
If I can get close I can tempt it
With some of the budgies' seed. There, I'm near,
But if it sang like that and I so close,
It would sear me, I think, to the bone.
It seems to love the glitter of the chain.

THE BIRD SAYS:

I will sing again for the chain.

THE METALSMITH
SAYS:

It can talk! Oo's a pretty . . . Oh
The chain. It is my chain.
Yet it is not my chain;
It is everything I own.
I borrow the gold and pay the debt back
By transforming the gold into a noble work.

THE BIRD SAYS:

I will sing again for the chain.

THE METALSMITH
SAYS:

If they sold me up it wouldn't pay for the chain.
And they'd put me in debtor's prison.
They would forge me an iron chain.

THE BIRD SAYS:

I will sing for the gold chain.

The Juniper Tree

THE METALSMITH
SAYS:
Look how it stretches out its great blue-sheened
    claw.
All right then. What's a little gold more or less?
I'll get another commission, to pay off on this one,
And another, to pay that off, and so on
And so on, down the line until it's time
To die and cheat the last customer.

Yet my work by this song
Will be so exquisite I shall have a patron by then.
I hang the chain on your claw, bird,
Sing for me again!

THE BIRD SINGS:
By my father devoured,
By my sister dined upon,
Butchered by my stepmother, digested by her,
Gathered in my half-sister's
Fine silk scarf,
Fine silk scarf.
She picked up the bones of me,
Did Anne-Marie,
And laid them inside the juniper tree.
I am become a great bird accordingly,
In plumage like fire! Like furnace gold!
Like brave blood! Like fresh leaf
Reborn from my true mother's tree
In gold! In fresh leaf!
In wildfire! In song!

*

THE COBBLER
SOLILOQUISES:
I think I am the only cobbler to craft
Shoes with toes; I believe they will become fashion-
    able:
I will create them ornamented with feathers
For they arise out of my fondness for birds.
Real birds, not like that metalsmith's aviary of tin
    fowl.
I often think that the foot is like a bird
Hopping along, pecking at the ground
And, poor thing, how can it stand steady without
    toes

Or, better, claws to grip the earth?
I have cages full of flesh and blood singing birds
From which I will model my fine slippers.
And I have just finished emptying my largest cage
Of tropical song-birds because there is standing
Outside on the window-ledge a remarkable fowl,
A kind of firebird of colours, a firework of a bird,
That will get me the king's leg.
If I lower my cage on him I will be made.
So gently with the window-sash and –

THE BIRD SINGS: *My father gnawed my bones,*
My stepmother sipped my marrow,
My half-sister picked me from her teeth
And gathered the bones of me,
The bones of me,
In a fine silk scarf,
Did Anne-Marie,
And put me inside the juniper tree
To lie with my true mother,
I am become a great bird accordingly
In plumage like soldiers' blood, like fresh leaf,
Like furnace gold, like ruby and like sunset.
Reborn from my mother's tree
In gold! In verdure!
In wildfire! In song!

THE COBBLER   Oh, sing again bird, sing again.
SAYS: While you're singing I tremble
               So I can hardly stand
               But if you do not sing
               I think I could cage you, yet
               I want you to sing.

THE BIRD SAYS: I will sing for those sky-coloured shoes.

THE COBBLER   What! the sapphire slippers?
SAYS: Those are the duke's. I do not own them
               Though I made them. He handed me a supple hide
               And told me it was his uncle's, whose title he has,
               And his feet only felt comfortable
               When they were trampling on his uncle.

I cannot give you the duke's uncle!
He would have my skin, though I doubt
If he'd feel comfortable cobbled in a cobbler.
I have dyed them a royal hue.

THE BIRD SAYS: I will sing for the sky-shoes.

THE COBBLER
SAYS:
All right. Done. I'm done too
But I must hear that song. If the duke looks
For his uncle's tattoos, I will explain
They got lost in the selvage, and use a doe's
 skin.
If I could learn that song I could persuade
Anybody of anything.

THE BIRD SINGS: *My father devoured me,*
My stepmother stewed me,
My half-sister's tears salted me
And she gathered me up,
Gathered me up,
In her fine silk scarf
And laid me inside the juniper tree.
I am become a firebird accordingly
In voice like gold and in plumage of fresh leaf
In plumage of sapphire of furnace gold
Of royal blood and fresh leaf
In wildfire of song.

*

THE MILLER'S
MEN CHANT:
Twenty miller's men
Hewing a black stone
Clickety-clack of the mill
Chip-chop at the stone
Our mill-wheel of granite
Fired at the earth's focus
Round as the sun
Pierced at the centre.
The stone months in the carving;
Ground in black granite
The warm loaves of new bread
Will steam like babies' breath.

THE BIRD SINGS: *My stepmother boiled me*

The One Who Set Out to Study Fear

My father devoured me.

THE MILLER'S
MEN SAY
SEVERALLY:
Why have you stopped?

Quiet! You can't hear it
With all that hammering.

FIFTEEN OF THE
MILLER'S MEN
RESUME HAM-
MERING, AND
CHANT:
The job's nearly finished –
Fifteen miller's men
Hewing a millstone
Clickety-clack of the mill
Chip-chop at the black stone
Our mother earth
Grinds the whitest flour
With solid thunder
Star-bright flour;
Black stone round as the sun
Pierced through your centre,
The families feed on new bread
As feathery and warm as baby-skin,
Ground in the stern surfaces.

FIVE MILLER'S
MEN SAY:
Do be quiet, and listen! . . . the bird
On the linden tree yonder.

THE BIRD SINGS:
My sister's tears
Salted my bones
And she gathered me up . . .

TEN OF THE
MILLER'S MEN
RESUME HAM-
MERING AND
CHANT:
Nearly finished –
Ten miller's men
Hewing their new stone
To bed in the mill
Pierced through the centre
Grinding the ages
Of wheat sprung from the earth
Earth grinds upon earth
The mill whitens like frost
Good bread on the table
White as child-flesh.

THE BIRD SINGS:
My sister drank my marrow,
Buried my bones deep
In my mother juniper's marrow.

ANOTHER OF THE MILLER'S MEN SAYS:	That bird! Hush – Your hammering will scare it. How can you work When it is singing?
THE REMAINING FIVE OF THE MILLER'S MEN RESUME HAMMERING AND CHANT:	Nearly finished – Five miller's men Have hewed the new stone That round as a black sun Pierced through the centre Grinds white lightning With granite thunder For all to feed.
THE BIRD SINGS:	*I am become a great bird accordingly* *My plumage gold as the wheatfield* *Rosy as soldier's blood; I sing* *Clothed in gold like sun-blood.*
A MILLER'S MAN SAYS:	Bird! Sing again as I work, Join with my work-song, Add your magic to the stone; I am the only one left working!
THE REMAINDER OF THE MILLER'S MEN SAY:	Bird! Sing as we rest So your symphony May recreate us!
THE BIRD SAYS:	Give me the stone when it's made.
ALL THE MILLER'S MEN SAY:	Our stone – our living!
ONE MAN SAYS (AFTER A PAUSE):	Maybe the old one is good enough for us.
ANOTHER MAN SAYS:	To know that song for ourselves – All work would be pleasure thereafter, We could with ease carve another.
ALL THE MEN CHANT:	Great navel-stone Round as the sun Life-work of twenty men Collar fit for an extraordinary bird Who wears a gold chain

Who flies in blue slippers –
Set the beam
The stone is completed
Raise the stone
Heave-ho heave-ho
Raise the stone
As the granite moon rises
Let the bird
Fly through its centre
Carry the stone off
Light as a thundercloud;
Work will be pleasure
Having heard that song, ever after.

THE BIRD SINGS: *My father devoured me,*
My stepmother butchered me,
My half-sister drank me up
And took my bones,
And took my bones,
Enfolded in fine silk
To the juniper tree.
I became a great bird accordingly,
Reborn from my mother tree
On my errand I fly.
I am complete for the task –
A gold chain, sapphire slippers
And a millstone collar.

*

NORMAN SAYS: Oh, I feel as though a weight
Has been lifted from my heart
Oh, quite suddenly, as though a stone
Was lifted from my shoulders.
I feel wonderfully good.

EVE SAYS: That's strange. I feel terrible.
Is there thunder coming?
I heard the roof-tree creaking
As though a heavy weight had settled there.
Something that should be flying
Has settled on our house.

118

NORMAN SAYS: It's strange, I feel wonderfully good.
                It can't be thunder!
                The sun's shining! I feel as though
                I were going to meet a friend.

EVE SAYS: I feel buried alive.
                Anne-Marie weeping in the hearth
                Among the ashes
                Makes it no better
                Weep, weep, weep.
                Can't you smile and make us all feel better?
                I would cry if I could.

NORMAN SAYS: Anne-Marie must be letting go of all her sorrow
                In one hour of her young life.

EVE SAYS: Then why does my sorrow
                Feel like thunder that won't break?

NORMAN SAYS: Listen? Isn't that singing
                Far above?

THE BIRD SINGS: *My stepmother butchered me . . .*

EVE SAYS: Singing? There's an ugly howling
                From the approaching storm.
                God, I must get this top off –

NORMAN SAYS: You've ripped your best dress!

THE BIRD SINGS: *My father devoured me . . .*

NORMAN SAYS: I do believe that is the bird
                My friend the cobbler told me about
                That sings so sweetly, they are words
                If I could hear them. I'm going outside.
                The sun's shining, it is warm
                The whole world smells of – I don't know –
                Cinnamon. I'm going outside.
                Come outside, Anne-Marie,
                Leave your weeping,
                I think that bird is calling.

EVE SAYS: Don't go, husband, don't go.
                I feel my head is bursting.
                I feel the house is about to burst into flames.

NORMAN SAYS FROM THE DOOR:	There – do you hear it?
THE BIRD SINGS:	*Anne-Marie* *Gathered the bones of me,* *The bones of my life,* *And tied them in her silken scarf* *To lay them inside the juniper tree.*
NORMAN SAYS:	Look what the bird has given me! It just dropped out of the sky!
ANNE-MARIE SAYS:	Father! That golden chain round your neck – It makes you look like a king!
EVE SAYS:	Oh God, bury me. The thing has come for me.
NORMAN SAYS:	Come out into the sun, Eve. Look at this wonderful chain The bird has given me.
EVE SAYS:	I know why you are weeping now, Anne-Marie. I will weep with you in the ashes.
THE BIRD SINGS:	*My stepmother dismembered me,* *My half-sister, Anne-Marie,* *Gathered the bones of me,* *I am become a great bird accordingly.*
ANNE-MARIE SAYS:	I can't stay weeping indoors all day. I hear the bird calling too. I will go outside to find out What it will do to me.
ANNE-MARIE SAYS (FROM OUTSIDE):	Glorious bird, sing my sin aloud!
THE BIRD SINGS:	*I was reborn from my mother tree* *Because my sister took pity on me.*
ANNE-MARIE SAYS:	Look, Father, it has given me Magic shoes, sapphire, with sapphire stones, Slippers like bird-claws Which fit perfectly. See how I can leap and dance in them!

	See how they grip. Oh I am so happy.
NORMAN SAYS:	I'm happy too, my dear.
ANNE-MARIE SAYS:	You shall be the Lord Mayor, in that gold chain. I felt so sad before I went outside. Now – everything is warm And smells of cinnamon. Mother – come outside, Be happy with us.
EVE SAYS:	No! I tell you it's the end of the world. You are playing with electricity. That galvanic bird settled on our roof-tree Is what they call the Devil. Its howl electrifies me. Look, My hair. It is standing on end. I must get earthed. I will roll in the ashes. That's safe, a coating of ashes.
THE BIRD SINGS:	*My false mother devoured me* *My false mother butchered me* *My false mother drank me up* *My false mother cut my head off.*
EVE SAYS:	I must get outside. The chimney is telling my sins over and over. It is the bird singing. His words Are magnified by the hearth-back. They will sound softer under the wide sky I am through the door – The house is burning, it is burning! No, it is the bird on the roof-tree. It has hellfire for feathers. It is throwing A black moon at me!
NORMAN SAYS:	Mother! Wife! A great stone, a black meteorite Has fallen from heaven and squashed her. A thundering great millstone. I can see her blood Bubbling through the centre-hole, But look who's here, coming through the steam

and the smoke.
He mustn't see the blood or the splashed brains.
Victor! Are you back, then?
Did you enjoy your visit with your great-uncle?
He is a great classical scholar, they tell me.
Come in and let's have supper.
I want you to decline
The verb *amo, amare* for me.

Ashiepaddle

Ashiepaddle

My new daughters are strangers to me. Such questions!

'Are you very, very rich, Daddy?'

Stupid child. She has only to look around. We pick our way through the knot-garden. There is an enormous hagstone by Henry Moore in the very centre, settled among white roses.

'How rich are you, Daddy?' That's Dowsabell. She has a military mind. And a hooked nose like the Duke of Wellington. I am enormously rich, of course. But the money is tainted.

'Very, very rich. But I wish you would call me Step-daddy. Or by my own name, Alexander.'

'That's a great name. But may I call you General?'

They call me General Midas behind my back. It's not quite an honorary rank. I was a full colonel when we pillaged the women's city and brought back so much gold with blood on it, and a woman apiece. The women are all dead now.

'I want to be an archbishop like my daddy was.'

That's Clare, the bookish one. Yellow papery skin. Black snapping eyes. Ah, Ash, Ash, that's all you are now. I will not snap at these ugly children, for your sake.

'But, dear Clare, they don't ordain women.'

'Then I will marry an archbishop.'

'You will marry the Church and I will marry the army, a general, like our new daddy.'

Dowsabell tilts her beak and Clare flutters her eyes like a scholar riffling crisp pages, and they both link their arms in mine as we come out into the avenue of closely pleached yews that is like a dark corridor in a haunted house. An apparition melts through those apparently solid walls. It is a young girl in white. She stands in our way for a moment, and then disappears as quickly as she came. In white, yes, but strangely written-upon. Wide blotches of mud disfigure her skirts. Her blonde hair is streaked and clotted with ashes.

'Ashiepaddle! Ashiepaddle!' shriek my two companions, jumping up and down and pointing at my true daughter, named like her mother, Ash. 'Ashiepaddle! Ashiepaddle!' They mock her with the name of scorn she gave herself.

A psychologist would say that I had laid up trouble for myself by remarrying too fast. But Ash became strange soon after her mother died. She deliberately does all the grubby work. On rising she puts on a fine white linen dress to carry and record all the grime of the day. So that about this time in the evening she is as we saw her just now, looking like the gardener's urchin, having converted her dress to filthy working-rags. Her chores in the house finished, she haunts the gardens and the grounds. She says she is not fit to visit nature without being dirty too.

'Look, she's left a trail of grime.' I kneel down and test the sooty grease that bedaubs the grass. 'Can't either of you control your step-sister?' There's no use asking their mother, my new wife. She is too busy with the building-works. Her plan is to build the new cathedral in our grounds.

'The servants are quite pleased,' says Dowsabell, 'that she does all the grimiest chores. They say she never goes to bed. They stay up late telling stories in the warm kitchen, and when the cook and the butler and the footman and the tweenies get sleepy and go off to bed, then Ashiepaddle starts scrubbing the stone floors and sweeping the stairs.'

'I had mislaid my copy of *Paradise Lost*,' says Clare. 'I looked everywhere, and then went to ask in the kitchen. I heard Ashiepaddle chanting: "So spake the Enemie of Mankind enclos'd/In Serpent, Inmate bad, and toward *Eve*/Address'd his way, not with indented wave,/Prone on the ground, as since, but on his reare,/Circular base of rising foulds, that tour'd/Fould above fould a surging Maze, his

Head/Crested aloft, and Carbuncle his Eyes;/With burnisht Neck of verdant Gold, erect/Amidst his circling Spires . . ." Then she saw me, and got up, and put my book face down on her chair, and slowly and deliberately lay down on the unswept floor, and writhed like a serpent keeping her arms straight at her sides until she had disappeared into the inglenook.' Clare's eyelids were going like a microfilm reader on fast forward. 'I didn't know where to look. Then the butler got up and handed me my book with a bow. I thanked him, and left.'

'I think you speak the Milton exceptionally well.' I intend the praise to calm her. 'What an excellent memory you have.'

'I like that serpent,' says Dowsabell, 'he is in his full-dress uniform, all gold wire and scarlet cloth and shining buttons and a leathery polished smell, like an infantry officer at a ball.'

'I have heard that at the end of the day she rips her clothes off and boils them white again in the kitchen copper, stirring it with a paddle like a naked witch. Then she sleeps all night in her skin in the warm ashes, enfolding herself in them, as if they were soft eiderdown. Therefore is she called Ashiepaddle. Then at dawn she runs out coated with grey ashes and plunges in the river, washing it all off, and runs back through the meadows in the buff.'

'Who told you that!' I am outraged.

'Jack the shepherd!' shriek the two girls together. Dowsabell takes up the story. Both girls are more animated than I have ever seen them before. They look almost – pretty? No, that couldn't be.

'Jack thought it was a spirit at first. A naked person running is always regarded as a spirit, and invisible. So he pretended not to notice, as was polite. But it got down among the buttercups, and rolled around in them. When it got up it was golden, and danced all around him, laughing, before it ran off leaving him gaping. Now he says it is a goddess. He has bought a banjo, and spends a lot of time in the field waiting for her to reappear, so he can play to her, and capture her in her dance with his music.'

I don't care for this one bit. At the very least, Ash is compromising her marriage prospects, if she has any left. 'Why a banjo?' I ask.

'A banjo is an instrument that can only be played fast,' replies Clare, dryly.

'She seems to keep everybody very happy and interested in life,' I say, looking at the girls' delighted blushes.

'The house runs like a dream. The staff won't let us lift a finger,' pouts Dowsabell.

'It's certainly nice to wake in winter and begin your reading with the fires going and the floor swept clean and the breakfast laid, as if by spirits.'

Clare, I think, had a notion that if she read enough books somebody would come along and ordain her. Dowsabell thought chiefly about her carriage, and stance, her deportment and her seat at horse; it was to give the best military expression to her Wellingtonian nose, which would otherwise have looked simply witchy. For myself, well, time passed in the company of my new wife like an irrelevance. There was this great project of the cathedral, but my role was chiefly signing cheques and approving loads of stone. The thousands of tons of stone and the hundreds of thousands of gold dollars they cost to be transported here, fitted together, sculpted, were unreal, as if in paying for it I somehow volatilised the material. I knew I was pining for another reality. Each cheque I signed was some kind of alkahest or universal solvent. The stones became sculpted walls, and were re-placed by more stones. I paid off builders, who were succeeded by fresh builders. I paid for Dowsabell's clothes and Clare's books. Edwina's great cathedral was like a great, loose-fitting grey overcoat she was somehow one day going to be able to wear. The more I gave everybody the more we all became like sad, clean, beautifully dressed ghosts in a house of happy servants and a delinquent daughter. As I said, the money was tainted.

'Ghosts of the house, ghosts of the garden.' Clare could sometimes read thoughts, a little.

'Talking about ghosts,' says Dowsabell, 'Ashiepaddle likes to haunt the Old Chapel, the one that burnt down. She has planted a little herb garden round her mother's grave.' ASH, says the headstone, just ASH.

'I expect Mother will dismantle that old ruin when she builds the new cathedral.' Since Clare can read minds, she knows how to be cruel. 'I wonder where she will move that grave.' I never go there myself.

Dowsabell can be quite crude, as befits the prospective wife of soldiers, 'unflinching', she calls it. 'Well, the rosemary in your lamb last night came from that grave.' I suppose I should find that disgusting. It feels a little holy instead. I meant to spend a night in vigil at Ash's mother's grave, but my new wife keeps me up late signing cheques. Ash-Ash – mother and daughter is one flesh.

'I'm not unhappy with . . .' I begin, when I notice Edwina has arrived. She's a large woman, but she has the trick of arriving silently. Her face is like stone.

'Nobody's unhappy in a Christian household.' Never leave doors open to unhappiness – that's one of her principles. 'It's time for Vespers. If you're going to marry archbishops and generals, children, you'll have to learn how to pray properly. As if you were an archbishop yourself, or a general at a military mass-funeral.'

Dowsabell is accustomed to not listening to her mother. 'Somehow, in all her dirt, Ash still looks like a princess,' she remarks wistfully.

Edwina won't have it. 'Just you forget the dirty little princess. I want you clean and bright for the party tonight.'

Dowsabell flashes back. 'Curates and subalterns!' She has a natural and acute consciousness of rank.

'Great things do from little curates grow!' says Edwina and, looking at me, 'I want you there, Alexander. You are the father of the brides.'

I was giving Mossy the gelding a bit of his head in the Long Meadow when I almost ran down one of those religious blackbirds. I would have liked to make a proper job of it. I was polite instead, as befits a young subaltern who is ambitious. That is how General Midas likes us to be.

'Whoa! I do beg your pardon, Reverend Canon. My apologies. My horse is too spirited. I doubt if he was properly cut.'

'My fault entirely. But you are too kind. I'm only the curate at St Economy-over-the-Weir. You can call me "Father".'

'Are you now! Off to the Great House. What's her name? Clare. The one who has a fetish for dog-collars. I bet you'd have to sleep in yours if you married her.'

'I think you could keep your coarse talk for the Mess, Lieutenant. I expect you're mounted on a similar errand. I've heard Dowsabell gets just as hot for a scarlet coat.' He was right. I had my dress-uniform in my saddle-bag.

'I like you, Reverend. Let me dismount and walk beside you. We'll go up there together, like comrades in arms in the war of the sexes. I think these projects of our military squire, the general, will lead to improvements, don't you? Frankly, that first wife was a liability.'

'I don't know much about all that. We were warned by the See to look out for pagan heresies in the neighbourhood.'

'I think that has gone with the first wife. She wrote books. I've got one at home. Not much in my line. A peculiar story of the unity of all

being and even the clouds being the letters of God's name, everlast-
ingly uttered; of life in death and death in life. A fragment of it
stuck in my mind ". . . that wonderful secret writing that one finds
everywhere, upon egg-shells, wings, in clouds, in snow, crystals and
the structure of stone, on water when it freezes, on the inside and
outside of mountains . . ." I wonder if she practised what she
preached. That is either witchcraft, or beauty. What would you chaps
call it?'

'As it happens, I am training for the Holy Inquisition. Pure witchcraft. The Diocese is less concerned now she's dead.'

'If she is dead. Her own beliefs . . .'

'I won't bandy words. She's dead. And the squire's match with the
archbishop's widow is uncommonly sound. It will bring Church
and the military establishment back into proper alignment with the
landowning classes.'

'And the prospect of other marriages, such as our own . . .'

'Will cement the alliance.'

'With no more rumours of witchcraft.'

'Indeed, it is the worst heresy.'

'Good. Whoa boy!' My horse had shied at somebody or something
running behind the hedge, and was whinnying and dancing on its
hooves. I called out.

'Here you!' A rather formal, light and confident voice replied.

'What is your desire?' it said. And out came an incredible little
figure, in stained rags and with hair braided in mud, or something
worse. She, if it was a she, scampered out under the low boughs like
a monkey.

'My name is Ashiepaddle,' it said.

The curate was up to the occasion, as an incipient inquisitor. He
adopted an hauteur.

'Very well, girl,' he said, 'and what do you do? Are you a dustperson?'
She smiled back at his sneer. She was mocking, I could tell, but in a
strange way deeply sincere as well. Her quick eyes, the dirt and her
graceful movements added up to courteous irony.

'I tell fortunes.' She winked. 'Cross my palm with silver.'

'Fortunes? How do you tell fortunes?' I saw he was picking out
points in his interior *Malleus Maleficarum*.

'I watch the earth on graves, for what grows there. I watch how the
trees grow, for they are spirits. I consider how the rank dank earth
smells are transmuted to the perfumed hormones of grass and the

blessed crops. I watch the dirty, unregarded things. The maggots seething in the dustbins. The worms writing in the dust among the stones. I watch the turn of the tides and all complex non-linear systems and how the moon fattens and slims the forest steams. I tell fortunes by the stains of earth on my body and clothes. By the earth of my body. By the excrements that are hair, and nails, and blood, and dust and ashes. All the disregarded things cast away by the clean-living.'

This made sense. A battle was like an almost-random splash of men chucked over a disputed terrain. In a sense, all the forces of the universe were present, deciding the outcome. Besides, Ashiepaddle looked sexy, like a dirty gypsy. I looked down at my field-uniform. Soldiers dressed in khaki, didn't they, to go unnoticed about the terrain; pronounce it kackie.

'Tell my fortune,' I said.

'Really, Lieutenant!' I saw a drawn old inquisitor lurking behind the father's fresh young face. I had better not show him I'm at all serious.

'It's all right, Father. This kind of thing amuses me. Clausewitz used to consult clairvoyants; they have their ear to the ground, he said. Tell my fortune, O Chloe of the rubbish-dumps. Will I marry?' As I asked my question, a mistlethrush perched on a hawthorn branch fluted three bars of song. It's strange how that bird's song has its own inbuilt misty echo. Ashiepaddle was silent until bird and echo had finished.

'You will,' she said.

'Will it be a good marriage?' Again the bird gave out its three bars.

'It will.'

'And who will I marry?' This time the thrush prefaced its music with a sharp *tseep tseep*.

'A woman half-blind and bleeding.'

'I don't think that's my style at all.' I was turned off. Pity, she'd almost had me believing. The father looked contemptuous.

'Serves you right for dabbling. These people like to catch you with a riddle. Their stock-in-trade is very limited, but they like to vary it from person to person, to add profundity. Look, I'll show you. Ashiepaddle, can you tell my future simply by looking at me?' Again we heard the bird's little snatch of song.

'Yes, I can,' said Ashiepaddle. 'It is the same as the soldier's.' That was one in the eye for him. He was quite cross.

'You can be put in jail for fortune-telling! How should I ever marry a half-blind woman!'

'We stand under a tree. The birds in the tree have the sight. They tell me. Quarrel with the birds, not me.'

'You claim to know the speech of the animals, like the blessed Saint Francis?' The incipient inquisitor was back.

'Hardly anybody pays attention to the animals. I do. I listen, that's all.' The father began swelling like a toad.

'Satan is your counsellor, and a lie, and the father of lies,' he croaked.

'You mean the horned fellow with the shaggy flanks. He is a companion of my dreams in the dark of the moon. He is human and he is animal and he has a star in his brow, man-sphinx.' Ashiepaddle is a tease, I thought, but take care, sweet strange girl, take care. She'd got the father's goat, as they say.

'Satanism, heresy! Women have been burned for saying less. Burned to ashes, Ashiepaddle.'

'The ashes and the cinders of our martyrs cry out against your religion.' Both were deadly serious now.

'Martyrs! Do you mean witches?'

'I mean priestesses. I dress in ashes to remember them. And the ashes cry out.'

'I'll chastise you to death for this.' The priest gripped his stick hard. I noticed it was an ashplant. I gripped his arm.

'Steady, man! Let me take your stick. We don't want a bloody brawl on the highway.' The bird sang its sweet rapid notes again, and the priest stared round, aghast.

'She's gone! Where is she? I didn't see her go.' Nor did I, but I wasn't letting on.

'She hopped behind the hedge again as that bird called, like some kind of scudding bird herself,' I told him. I thought first aid was in order, so I got my flask out of the pack. The father had no prejudice against drinking – it might give you strange thoughts but it wasn't heretical – so discussing the theology of Bacchus, and consulting the flask frequently, we made our way up to the Great House. The butler showed us to a lobby where I could change and the father could wash his face and have a general brush down. When we joined the party the priest was full of our encounter.

'We had a curious experience on the way here . . .' He had trapped our hostess, a very large, very still woman, with an expression as settled as stone.

'We met a hedge-witch, who harangued us under a tree. She told us . . .'

'Steady,' I whispered. I wanted him to remember we were running in the marriage stakes ourselves. Ashiepaddle's dismal prediction would be less than tactful. Madame General Edwina seemed interested, however.

'What did she tell you?'

'Nothing of consequence . . .' but the father chipped in before I could stop him.

'She was a curious little figure in terribly stained clothes, and with ashes on her face. She looked like somebody who had been partly burned.' There was no movement about the statue of Madame Edwina to tell that our grotesque adventures would be in our disfavour, yet I knew. I think she emitted dilute I-am-always-slightly-offended-gas. She did, however, also speak.

'This . . . creature. Did she tell you her name?'

'It was Ashiepaddle. Do you know her?' Edwina now positively reeked of disapproval. But she was still the great stone face.

'I? Know her? No, not at all. A local character, I believe. I was told she likes to waylay wedding parties to, as she calls it, bless the bride.' She spoke as stone would speak, very heavily and slowly, in blocks. I was glad that General Alexander had joined us, and was listening. He was dressed fittingly in blood, money, death, moonlight and rainbows: that is, in his full dress-uniform of scarlet, gold and black, with a powdered wig and ranks of medals. He spoke brusquely, which was a relief.

'She throws a little soot on the bride's white dress, crying out to the wedding party, "Children! The way is open!"'

That young soldier must learn not to stare so at his general. I could see myself reflected in his eyes, like a toy soldier. Both he and the priest seemed troubled by their encounter with Ashiepaddle. But Edwina's business took precedence.

'I had a visit from HRH's new equerry.'

'Well, my dear.'

'We discussed our scheme for reorganising and revivifying the state.'

'You want our marriage to be an example to the whole ruling class.'

'You have it, Alexander. Intertwining marriages between Church and military will create an exceptionally stable social and monetary structure.'

'I suppose the lower classes, including my common soldiers, will be forbidden to marry or even associate outside their spheres.' I couldn't rid my mind of the image of a toy general in scarlet, gold and black floating like a contact lens on the eyeball of a young and ambitious subaltern.

'They never wanted to associate with us, anyway.'

'Tell me, my dove, of what class is Ashiepaddle a member?'

'Clergy and state, state and clergy are what matter; spirituality and the power to defend it; religion and land. The equerry listened to what I had to say, and returned this morning. It was better than we could ever have anticipated. A new dimension.' I never knew anybody to speak with such animation and remain so still as Edwina. There was a faint, exciting scent in the air. 'HRH thought that his class should not close ranks, but that we should make a triple alliance, Church, military – and nobility.'

'Three people can't marry.'

'Don't be dense, Alexander. The landed gentry who have been soldiers in their time mate with the daughters of parsons. Like us.'

'I don't think you can call your first husband, a dead archbishop, a "parson"!'

'The offspring of such marriages, superb virgins like Clare and Dowsabell, will offer themselves, as it were, with all propriety, of course, to selection by a series of titled men, earls and barons.'

It bothered me that Clare and Dowsabell were not my natural daughters. I would have preferred a scheme like that for my own flesh and blood. But Ashiepaddle would never enter Edwina's calculations.

'Clare and Dowsabell are only stepdaughters, I know, but we all bear your distinguished name by adoption.' Clare had inherited her mind-reading trick from her mother, evidently.

'And what is HRH going to do to promote this reform?'

'He is going to hold a series of balls.'

'Now that is delightful. Where?'

'Why, here, my dear.'

'What, in my house?'

'Our house.'

'At whose expense?'

'You can't expect a royal to pay.'

'Here, and at my expense.'

'Just so.'

'For a pack of earls inbred and dukes penniless.'

'If that were all, it would still be worthwhile.'

'Is there more?'

'H R H himself will enter the marriage stakes at these balls.'

'Oh. And supposing he can't find anybody suitable?'

'It's our business to see that he does.' The girls had drifted up, called no doubt by the come-here-daughters-gas my wife was emitting without moving a muscle.

'Girls, I was telling the general that you will have temporarily to discourage your present suitors. Please keep them on a nice long lead, however. You have other fish to fry.' The girls understood the whole plot instantly, perhaps by gaseous diffusion.

'My curate lends me all manner of books, and he is very learned, but we have books at home,' said Clare smugly.

'It is time to perch in a taller family tree,' said Edwina, still as a caryatid. Dowsabell was a bit upset.

'My subaltern was to be promoted.'

'I doubt if he would have made duke,' said my connubial statue, and that was the end of it.

I don't remember the rest of the evening very clearly. I woke on the bed in my dressing-room, still in my regimentals. I heard the wagons assembling in the stableyard. Today was the day I had to go to the city, to buy everything for the three royal balls. I struggled into my riding gear, and got downstairs. The girls were already up, my two stepdaughters nearly invisible against the flowerbeds in their chintzy dresses, so they looked like floating heads. Ashiepaddle appeared shimmering in sheer dead-white in the arch of the kitchen door. For once I was up early enough for Ash to be presentable still, immaculate, before she acquired those universal stains.

'Ash,' I said, 'you look lovely in white.' The comment was a mistake.

'I am called Ashiepaddle,' she said, frostily. The other two drifted up like tropical fish swimming through the air.

'Well, girls – and Ashiepaddle – you know there is going to be a great party here, and I've got to go up to town to order and buy everything. I want to get something exceptional for you. Tell me what it should be.' I knew in advance what they would want – except that Ash – beg pardon, Ashiepaddle – was unpredictable.

'Dresses, gorgeous, glorious dresses. A different one for each night of the party!' That was Dowsabell, sure enough. Poor girl, whatever her brocades and satins, however flounced and furbeloved, the more elaborate her coiffure and costume, among all that *pompe* she'd still look *funèbre*, like Wellington lying in state, nose projecting. Did they have to break the general's nose to close the coffin?

'And you, Clare?' Her eyelids started up like a moth caught in honey.

'Pearls, pearls to sew on the dresses like webs full of dew, the library of the spider.' She'd caught the party-spirit, for once. 'And lots of books, Daddy, about the Church, and the princes of the Church.'

'What about you, Ash?'

'Ashiepaddle.'

'Ashiepaddle.'

'Nothing, thank you.'

'Nothing?'

'Nothing.'

'But you must have at least as much a something as your half-sisters. It's your privilege. Nothing will come of nothing.'

'Then I'll tell you my privilege. I want the tree belonging to the first twig that brushes against your hat as you turn the horses round to head home.'

'A tree! We have forests full of them.'

'I want that one tree, for my own.' And greatly to my surprise Ash walked up to me, put her arms round my neck and kissed me. I smelt the freshness of her breath, as if she had meadows growing inside her.

'Will you come to the party as a tree, Ashiepaddle?' said Dowsabell, beakily.

The journey was uneventful. I was carrying gold, so we had to be alert, and I rode with my sword drawn. This appealed to Dowsabell who came running to meet me as we passed the home farm, and told me I looked soldierlike. I pointed her in the direction of the first wagon, where I had put the clothes chest, and Clare too, who came running up behind her. There was a shadowy copse by the road and, within the copse, a darker shadow, which spoke.

'There is a little horse with nothing but a long ash tree tied to his back, the roots in sacking.'

'It is your ash tree.'

'Thank you, Father.' Ash came out of the trees and her dress was caked with wet mud. It looked as if she had been rolling in it. She went to the little horse and, after untying it from the train, led it away. She didn't kiss me this time, and I was glad of that. Clare tapped me on the shoulder. The two were prancing around, their new dresses held up against their bodies. They looked like clowns, after the simple perverse dignity of Ash's slim body in her clotted dress.

I knew she had a special purpose in requesting the ash tree, so I was not surprised when a few days later I found it replanted on my wife's grave in the Old Chapel. Now there was a tree to visit, like a tabernacle. It was once the custom to plant a tree on every grave, and thus our forests grew and were renewed. People would visit the forests to pray and to communicate with the ancestors, to comfort and be comforted by them. To speak to the newly-dead, you would visit the fringes of the forest, and the young, freshly planted trees. If you wanted to communicate with the great and grand ancestors, the old ones, then you would penetrate to the heart of the forest where the great old trees flourished in their deeper silences, and where the founding fathers and mothers had been buried. Some of those central trees in the round forest were more than two thousand years old.

Now as I sank to my knees under my wife's tree I wondered about the way the common people, who still followed this custom, experienced the presence of the dead, and took counsel of them; what it was like to talk with the departed ones under the godmother tree. Did they see an apparition of the departed? Did they hear the loved one's voice in the rustle of leaves or in a bird's call? I sank down within myself, silencing all questions. I became quiet, as well as alert. There was a sudden waft of an exquisite perfume, and I had a quick memory of Ash, my wife, laughing with her head turned back as she went up a flight of curving stairs ahead of me. I have noticed that scents sometimes have this almost-hallucinatory effect. I waited for more, but there was no more. Not yet. I touched the smooth ash-bark and smelt my hand. The tree was the source of that perfume. For a moment the tree had given me back my love by distilling a wonderful odour from her grave by the alchemy of its canopy, and so the two worlds met. So the dead live by mediation of branch, leaf and air, and the plants love to be loved and to be their messengers. Ash knew this, and by resuming the custom had opened the door again between the two worlds. My second wife believes that barbaric human voices reverberating in a stone forest built to shelter her ideas of God and family from the open sky will open this door too. But would I not do better to bury my tainted bloody gold in the ground so that it may be transmuted further into what is beyond price?

'I'm not going to any of the balls, and that's flat, Dowsabell,' said Ash.

'Ashiepaddle, it's a royal command.'

'I must say you look rather splendid in your new clothes, like trees in flower, and I hope you catch a demi-royal husband in them, but I'm still not going.'

'They'll throw you in jail. Some very good books have been written in jail.'

'I don't care, Clare. I like dungeons and caves, the dirtier the better.'

'Of course, the festivities are not at your clean time, are they, Ashie? However, if we all dance until dawn, we might stand a chance of seeing an inch of clean skin on you.'

'I'll go on one condition, Dowsabell.'

'Tell us.'

'Get a bowl of lentils.'

'Right-o. Lentils. Here, in this big jar.'

'And some dried peas. Mix them together. Now pour them on the ashes. Mix them in well. Now then, if I can't separate all the peas from the lentils clean out of the ashes by half-past three I won't go.'

'That's only five minutes!'

'Then I won't go. Look, I've started picking out the lentils. I can't possibly get it finished, can I?'

'Let's get Father. She's impossible.'

Ash grinned up at them from the ashes of the kitchen fire as they hurried off, leaving her to herself. This part of the old kitchen was roomy and well-lit with a vaulted timber roof and stone windows with window-seats; Ash would often sit there watching the pigeons in the yard or a swarm of meteors in the night sky. Just now there was an extraordinary activity at those windows and a fluttering shadow darkened the room. There was a tapping and an undulation of feathery bodies pressed up against the glass. Ash walked over and opened the windows and like a grey ragged angel the whole flock of pigeons swept in and settled round the hearth where the peas and lentils were scattered in the ashes. The beat of their wings made these soft ashes fly and the grey birds entered and left the grey cloud as if it was of their own feathery substance. Gradually the birds flew out by the same way they had come in and the grey dust settled. They had not eaten the peas or the lentils, but had left them in two neat piles on the stone hearth. The ash had flown everywhere, and was still settling. The girl knelt in front of the two piles of seeds, her fists clenched. The cooing of the doves hovered in the room, a soft *hriliu*, *hriliu*, which Ash knew was their sound of deep satisfaction.

'I'm not going,' she said, 'I'm still not going . . .'

I, General Patrick Fatprick Alexander, hide behind a stone and watch my errant daughter make perfectly sure she cannot go to the party, despite her rumoured vow over the peas and the lentils. In the ruined chapel (the chancel of which burgeons with the healthy growth of the ash tree that has grown so boldly since that daughter planted it on her mother's grave) young Ash makes a bonfire of her wardrobe and jewellery. She contrives a small grate of her wooden clothes-hangers. Upon this she arranges her shoes, the plain sensible ones she uses for walks, the boyish ones she had worn at school, the spangled evening shoes and the fashionable Roman sandals.

She sighs, and places on top of these her pink bedroom slippers, their rims lined with fur-fluff, and her long leather boots with the six-inch heels.

Within this pile of shoes she now tucks all her underwear: her plain white cotton knickers, her purple knickers edged with Honiton lace, her blue nylon knickers, her flowery Marks & Spark's ones, her black nurse's bloomers.

Then her bras, the white, the black, the French with lace; and her flesh-coloured tights, and two plain cotton vests left over from her schooldays.

On top of these flimsies, she arranges her jerseys and cardigans: her V-necked pullover in khaki cashmere, her black polo-necked jersey for riding, and the cardigan with the high-standing military-style collar.

Now she unscrews the paraffin can and pours oil over these garments. She gets up off her knees and goes back into the house. She comes out almost immediately with an armful of skirts, long tweedy skirts, a red velvet skirt with flounces at the hem, three mini-skirts, one polka-dotted in linen, a black formal skirt, three pairs of jeans and a pair of corduroy hotpants.

She throws them on the heap, and returns into the house. She brings out her blouses, flowered and plain, with puffed sleeves, severe pink blouses with button-down collars, classic paisley blouses, ruffled black silk blouses like theatre chocolates; the boy's cricket shirt she likes to wear in bed; three T-shirts decorated with the unsmiling faces of Beethoven, Sylvester the Cat and Elvis Presley. Lastly, she puts on top of the pyre her four white linen working-dresses.

Now she comes out with her other dresses, which she lays on the pyre, like a garnish: there is the blue voile dress with the pearl buttons, the little black Churchly dress, the long white one for summer parties, the lamé dress and the sober brocade, the thin good-weather cottons with their whirls and flowers, the warm navy-blue suit for the office, and two nylon nighties, one red, one black, each with stiff flowers on the bodice.

Now it is time to light the fire. The first three matches will not catch it alight, so she pulls out a pair of cotton pants which she dips in the paraffin to use as a spill; it flares up, and now there is no stopping the flames. The dresses writhe, trying to get free, her blouses raise their arms in despair, the crotch of her jeans charges itself with fire, the bras blacken like black nursing mothers and her working dresses become irretrievably African. The flames leap and weave for themselves a heavy hood of slaty smoke; they are now taller than she is. She pulls off her slippers and throws them in the fire. She pulls off her dressing-gown and throws that in as well, stands naked, basking in the good heat of her finery. Naked, ah, Ash, Ash, she resembles so closely her dead mother I cannot believe it is not she. It is witchcraft! I step out from behind my stone calling out to the woman I had first married.

'Ash! Your clothes! What have you done!'

'I'm dead, Alex,' she cries joyously, 'I don't need clothes any more. I'm everywhere!' and she steps into the fire. I run towards it to rescue her and my daughter Ash steps out of the conflagration's other side, slapping her hair at crown and crotch to put out the little flames. She passes by me and does not see me though her eyes are wide, and fades into the smoke which is now filling the little chapel like the coils of a monstrous basking serpent.

Ash says: 'I am about my mother's business. They can call it "witchcraft", if they like. It is not military, it is not clerical, and it is certainly not noble – so witchcraft for the remainder will do. As for sin – what sin is there in listening to the inspirations and improvisations of the natural world?

'There! Quite clearly and unmistakably, that little bird standing on a branch of my mother's glorious grave-tree sang *Look-look-look at me*, meaning *tree-with-bird* at that precise *moment*, in that *precise posture*, on that *actual twig* of the tree which has filled by its witchcraft that space in this world which my mother vacated.

'Spirits need no clothes, nor do those who converse with spirits. Skin is the dress in which we meet the gods. Therefore I assist my concentration by remaining skyclad, as they say, within the shelter of this tree which bodies forth my mother's name in its name and mine, Ash. *Look-look-look-at-me* and this is what the clothes I have discarded were saying, and the reason why they were discarded. Now the bird sings *Beblack beblack*. It is as I now know I must remain naked at all times for my work, whether it is housecraft or witchcraft, for a naked person in this land is regarded as invisible, as though their skin absorbed all visibility and they were black. Being black and clad like the night sky I have become clean too, like a spirit. I am become the very ghost of a black fairy, a piece of invisible night. The convention that they worship and which seals their eyes against all invisibles forbids their seeing or even looking at me as I run in my skin up and down stairs, bringing them their dishes and candles in my invisible hands. I have a free passage between two worlds, for when I wish to enter the social order I simply put on a dress, and I am in it immediately. My white working-dresses as they dirtied drew closer to freedom and invisibility, but now they are burnt to black cinders and there is no suitable dress within my knowledge that will admit me to that house as anything less than a spirit, or to those parties. There the people prance and simper, their exaggerating clothes echoing and anticipating every movement and quelling those not acceptable. They need the vents of big collars and the chimneys of immense sleeves in order to notice their own selves; only by abstraction and amplification can they envisage others; or by dotted pearls hypnotise with satin surfaces. *Be-black, be-black.* I wear my uterine skin to be near the sources of creation, and they can only see that as darkness. Darkness, and absence, an invisibility running skyclad through the house as it might be along the branches of this tree to learn, to learn . . .

'*Look-look-at-me* says the bird-with-tree, the grave-tree that has over the months grown and formed itself – I see now – into a perfect model of the spaces of the house bequeathed by my mother to my father, the general; just as the tree has replaced her absence, so has its wood clothed in leaves entered the social order, penetrating it by

141

twig and branch and constructing a solid negative or model in reverse. Where there are capacious rooms and empty halls, there is solid living wood; where there is bricks and mortar, open breathing air. That big knot is the front door in the buttress root and bole of the front hall; the trunk is the big winding main staircase; these branches give the patterns of the rooms *en suite*.

'*Look-look-look-at-me.* I can tell off the whole of my home in this tree. I have run since babyhood along every twig and corridor, up to the airy attic tiled with foliage. There is learned Clare's room where this bough turns and swells at the joint; fickle Dowsabell's playroom with the white bed and the tin soldiers where it rises and thins into the long narrow gallery with windows; and there's my father's spartan chamber in this straight bough; my stepmother's cathedral-like bedroom in this swollen gall.

'*Look-look-look-at-me.* And this solid map of my home in my underground mother's again-living flesh tells me once more what I had forgotten, her private apartments below ground-level, her forgotten cellar-room, her withdrawing rooms for magic that my father the general sealed-off and forbade her, and for which she pined to death, her subterranean spinning-room, her chambers of masks, her walk-in wardrobes of wonder-awakening dresses.

'*Be-black-black-black-black.* Those rooms in my tree-plans, where she herself lies within the magical soil putting on her new guises, are also in actuality here, below the cellarage of the house, thus I penetrate the dark rooms, crypt upon crypt, using no lights, just at each new archway pausing at the threshold to listen to the sound of the pitch-black space that opens before me, and by that resonance guiding my footsteps with echo and touch of air and the smell of stone and where it vaults or opens. This is why the earth called me, and the discarded, disregarded, dirty things, so that I would one day be able to navigate this underground darkness to my mother's domains. Now I can unseal these rooms because I can see the doors and their golden fastenings by body-light and as the new air rushes in the perfume long-pent in her dresses and implements is the sweetest air I have ever smelt and brings with it such light as seems to be turning on lamp after brilliant lamp in our new and old wonderland in the roots of the house and in the roots of the tree. Now I sit down at her immense dark mirror and learn to clothe myself anew, and enter the many worlds.'

She wears the long series of wonder-awakening dresses,
She wears the fishskin cloak,
She wears the gown of pearl with the constellations slashed into its
  dark lining,
She undresses out of the night sky, each night of the year a different
  sky,
She wears altitude dresses and vertigo dresses,
She plucks open the long staircase at the neck with the big buttons
  of bird-skulls in the white dress of sow-thistle.
She has leather breeches known to be chimp-skin,
She has combed star-rays into a shaggy nightdress,
She has a bodice of bone-flounces, a turbinal blouse through which
  the air pours.
There is a gown she has that shimmers without slit or seam like the
  wall of an aquarium;
A starfish moves slowly on its pumps across her bosom,
A shark glides, a turtle rows silently between her knees,
And she adopts in turn the long dress of sewn louse-skin,
The rompersuit of purple jam packed with tiny oval seeds,
The foggy grey dress, and lapping between its folds
Bird-cries and meteor-noises and declarations of love echo;
The ballgown of ticker-tape;
The evening dress of flexible swirling clockwork running against time;
The cocktail dress of bloody smoke and bullet-torn bandages;
And the little black dress of grave-soil that rends and seals as she
  turns.
Often she sits up all night in the general's library
Sewing strong patches from his wardrobe of military thought
Into her wounded dresses.

'I think you've done exceptionally well, General,' said the prince, 'a
glittering occasion.'
  'Thank you, Your Highness.'
  'You have transformed this old house. I have never seen so much
food, and so ingeniously served. That great pasty with five courses in
it, for instance, starting with hors-d'oeuvres, chopped egg, whitebait
and, in compartments of the crust, cold white wine; giving way,
like eating an edible railway train, to minced steak Diane, and fine
burgundy; and eventually dwindling down to *bombe surprise* with
ice-cream on the inside and champagne encircling, finishing up with

coffee and liqueurs built discreetly into the caverns of pastry. That is remarkable domestic technology, in my opinion, to utilise the natural insulating properties of baked crust to keep cold food cold and hot food hot. You even used a vacuum layer for the ice-cream, and that was confirmed when his *bombe* exploded over my equerry's new uniform. Everybody was so embarrassed he became almost invisible for a moment, but it made me laugh heartily.'

'Your Highness's generous hilarity saved the situation. I am most grateful.'

'Good job it wasn't me, eh?'

'Unthinkable, Highness. I hope everything will content you. In all respects. I hope Your Highness will be satisfied. With the company.'

'What? Oh, the women. Just like me! Rabbiting on about the technology of pasties and forgot the most important thing. The women. The glittering, tittering women. Well. They are certainly delightful to look at, General.'

'Will you take the first dance, Prince?'

'Naturally. That will be with my host's eldest daughter.'

'Excuse me, Highness, my elder stepdaughter, Clare.'

'Clare. Enchanted. Stepdaughter. A tragedy in the family, General?'

'I fear so, Highness.'

'I had heard. Mother and daughter gone, eh?'

'Something like that, Your Excellency.'

'Left you a packet, they tell me. Steady! *Who* is that magnificent black woman in white! She shines and whispers. I never expected . . . in the provinces . . . some princess . . . Madame General, you must know who she is!'

'It is a mask, Your Highness. Some perfectly ordinary woman underneath it.'

'Ordinary? I will dance with her and find out whether she is ordinary. Let the band strike up!'

I swear I saw Edwina stagger – just a millimetre or so – when the prince took that stranger-woman in his arms. She was certainly an eyeful. Whoever it was had had the chutzpah to put on a full white high-necked dress and on top of that the face-mask of a black woman with red lips under a mountainous coiffure of snow-white hair. She was now gripping the prince with small black-gloved hands, which showed up a treat on his white and gold uniform. His boots were as black and glossy as the mask. They were in deep conversation, and at one point the prince rapped his partner's face with his knuckles. By custom, the band was obliged to continue until the prince stopped dancing. They had struck the note with Offenbach's *Barcarolle*, so now they were stuck with it, like a perpetuum mobile.

'Close up you can see it's a mask. If I rap it – please permit me – it gives a hollow papier-mâché sound. You are somewhere beneath the blackness. When you dance, you move like a wet dream . . . Not even that royal obscenity causes you to falter. I have never before danced with a woman who did not miss her step when I said that. It is my command that you speak to me. But you won't, I know. Therefore we must continue to dance. Under this glossy black, what is your true colour? Either you speak, or we dance on for ever.' The tall willowy prince and his mystery-partner with the coal-black face and hands whirled on in a complex figure of black, white, red and gold.

'He's extremely discourteous.' Edwina was the only still thing in the room whirling with dancers. The dance floor filled with couples and emptied again as they grew exhausted, while the prince and his anomalous partner danced on.

'A prince can't be discourteous, my dear, by definition. It is in his courts by his courtesy that law and custom are created. What he says goes.' As I snapped back at Edwina the clocks began to chime midnight, and the band faltered. I saw the prince's strange partner tear herself away from him, I saw her scudding away among the other women, and then she turned round in the crowd so I couldn't see her anywhere. The prince came striding up to me. He was sweating. Royals never sweat, any more than they carry money.

'I'd know her anywhere,' he said, taking me by the arm and leading me along the line of curtsying women. His superb black leather boots kicked something which was rolling on the floor. He bent and picked it up. It was the black mask. There were diamond and pearl pendants still fastened to the cardboard earlobes.

'Highness, she has dropped her mask and merged with all the other white-clothed women.'

'Damn and blast!' he cried out, surveying the women, who cowered.

Courtesy decreed that when a prince swore, then everybody present should echo him, since, if he did, it was no longer a sin or a solecism, but a custom and courtesy.

'Damn and blast!' said everybody.

When the prince came down to breakfast he refused the orange-juice, porridge, fried-egg-and-bacon, toast-and-marmalade pasty waiting for him in its spotless napkin, and so everybody had to go hungry. The girl who was serving was naked, so I couldn't see who it was. I made a note to tell the cook to ensure that her girls wore an apron at least in the future. His Highness was very low.

'I am depressed by last night. Particularly by your ignorance of who this woman might be.' The prince absent-mindedly helped himself to salad from the bowl offered by the invisible servitor.

'Thank you.'

'*De nada. El pan comido y la compañia deshecha.*'

The prince took a mouthful of lettuce very distantly. Everybody now had salad, but courtesy decreed that nobody ate breakfast faster than royalty did. I remembered how, one day as he left the court at Versailles, St Simon paused to watch a dog gnawing a bone, and rejoiced to see genuine emotion. The prince put his fork down.

'I didn't know it was the custom hereabouts for buffet breakfast to be served by topless, indeed, everythingless women. Not quite charming, when you're eating perhaps. Though, strangely, I am not very hungry today. I wonder why.'

I found it very difficult to explain so natural a custom.

'Nude, Highness . . . I really . . . We have a slight servant problem . . . we are so accustomed . . . very shocking, no doubt . . . when a servant has insufficient funds for good clothes we allow her to wear her skin as best, and treat her as an invisible person. So ingrained is this habit in us that I was quite taken aback to realise that our custom would present no impediment to Your Highness's vision.'

'Well, she's gone now. There is a slight, very pleasant odour about this food. It reminds me, ah, I have it! of the smell inside the black pasteboard mask my elusive lady left behind. It's damnable, here is her smell, but where is she! An invisible lady indeed, my Lady of the Night, but here, right here in this room with her tantalising scent. Well, General, what are you going to do about it!'

'Another ball, Highness, there is another ball tonight.'

And there was. I remember it only in its fragments, but it was an equal disaster. Indeed the woman came, manifesting herself out of whatever invisibility she hid in, but tonight she wore the mask of a mulatto, the broad features and tawny skin equally fascinating. The prince was as before thunderstruck, or I should say cuntstruck.

As the couple began dancing again, I ordered my stepdaughters'
ex-suitors, Lieutenant Whatever-it-is and Reverend Nobody, to watch
out and stop the woman escaping. It ought to have been easier, because
this time her gown was peach-coloured. Then the chimes struck, and
the orchestra wheezed into silence, and the prince staggered as the
woman pulled herself away. But the rest of the dancers had formed a
circle and when the prince called out 'Detain that woman' they closed
their ranks to her and snatched at her face and gown and somehow,
I still to this day can't say, she melted away from them, though the
prince had gone quite scarlet and was stamping his feet and pointing
and calling out, 'There she goes, streaking down the stairs.' Later, I
learnt that up country 'streaking' was the term for running nude on
to a football pitch, or through a courtroom during the course of a
trial, or up the aisle during Holy Communion, for sheer exuberance
during the dog-days.

As the prince stood fuming encircled by my guests, they came up
one by one and offered him remnants of the evening's passion. A pair
of tawny gloves, a peach-coloured ballgown, a papier-mâché mulatto
mask with the hair attached.

'Damn and blast!' he said, letting the empty clothes fall.

'Damn and blast!' echoed everybody.

There was a replay of that breakfast too. I was aware that my household
had only the three chances, and the prince had addressed no more
than a few formal words to my stepdaughters so far. His thoughts
were entirely taken up with the changeable blackness of the mysterious
woman. I thought I heard Ash's voice whispering, but when I looked
round there was nobody there.

'Some fruit, Highness, with your breakfast?'

The prince turned and plainly saw somebody or something, for his
eyes widened and he smiled.

Then he shut them again, and laid his hands over them, still
smiling.

'An invisible breeze, bearing grapes. It is not considered good
manners to look at an invisible person, and I am supposed to be Mr
Manners himself. But thank you.'

'Don't mention it,' said Nobody.

The replay of the breakfast gave way to a replay of the ball, but
now everybody was expecting the fascinating stranger to arrive, like a
compound familiar ghost. Her face was negroid, as before, but the

skin was only faintly beige, and the dress was a deep night-purple. Somebody suddenly realised that they were standing next to the visitant, and drew aside; then everybody drew aside, and she was left standing in the middle of the floor as the prince, still black-shod and in his white and gold uniform, advanced on her, his white-gloved hands held out in welcome. The prince was smiling and the mask was smiling too, so they were the only cheerful-looking ones in the room of sour faces.

'You are as beautiful as ever, whatever your disguise,' said the prince in clear and resounding royal tones. 'Your mask tonight – would you call it high yaller? Or is it octoroon?' Then they were dancing.

And were still dancing when the midnight chimes sounded. Everybody stopped to watch and listen to the couple in the centre. I had spoken to all the men; they were to prevent the woman escaping; at sword-point if need be.

'Midnight already? Stay and be my bride. I will otherwise never marry. My line will die with me.'

Then the woman spoke for the first time. Her voice was loud, clear and had a curious resonance. When I came to examine the three masks closely I found that they were constructed with internal sound-boxes in the moulding to enlarge the voice, like the personae of Greek and Roman actors.

'I will be your bride,' she declared, 'if you can catch me.'

But this time we were ready for her, and she knew it. She retreated to the long windows, which were open on the evening sky. Her dress merged with the purple of it, and in that instant I knew we had lost her. I ran forward into the darkness and saw the full moon setting behind the Old Chapel, casting a white path on the dew of the grass, which slowly faded. I picked up the octoroon mask, and handed it to the prince, who raised it to his nostrils. He was furious and ice-cold, the willowiness now gone, unbending, he walked like a master at sword. I wished I had him under command, I could have trained him to be a soldier indeed. Now he was commander-in-chief through and through.

There was no regret in his voice when he spoke. Only determination.

'I am left with an empty mask, which smells of the night air. I cannot marry a mask, or the night air. Take note that this is my proclamation. Sound, trumpet!'

The orchestra was caught on the hop there, but the trombonist managed a passable fanfare.

'*Primus*. Any woman whom these masks fit perfectly will be my bride! *Secundus*. All marriage and giving in marriage will cease until I have my bride. Sound, trumpet!'

The trombone fastened his golden seal on the prince's ringing, irrevocable words.

What could we say? We all said it.

'Damn and blast!'

I thought that it would be fairly easy to find the woman, even if we did have to search the entire kingdom. The skull of whoever it was who wore these masks was remarkably small, and the eye-sockets were so widely spaced that an ordinary person would not be able to see out of them very well. The resonant chambers that magnified the voice were set in certain mouldings which made the fit absolutely individual.

I explained this to Edwina, who wore a stone mask I knew was a face. She was all for quick action, and called Clare in from her reading.

'How do you know only one woman wore them? It could have been three separate people. Clare, I am sure the octoroon mask will fit you.'

'No, mother, my eyes are too big and too close.'

'That is why I have brought the surgeon, my dear.' Edwina had the only logical solution. I had wondered what the surgeon–barber was doing there. My head had been shaved for my party wig only this week, and nobody, so far as I knew, needed a tooth pulled. Clare began to protest. She was not my daughter, but I began to tremble.

'I am quite sure this will fit you. Look, I have taken a moulding of the mask.' She picked the face of our visitant out of a velvet bag and held it up. The plaster was white as the full moon I had seen presiding when she escaped. We were about to fake a dolly-imitation of our prince's lover.

'If we had room just here, my dear,' said Edwina, 'in the socket.'

'My eye!'

'You can read just as well with one, and nobody insults a one-eyed princess.'

'Mother!'

'Your knife, Surgeon–barber. Drink this, my love. It will numb the pain.'

The prince had quite recovered his spirits, and had taken over my ballroom for his durbar. Everybody was aware, however, of the air of danger which had settled round him. His gracious manner was on a short fuse. The masks were to be tried in reverse order.

'And who is next for the mask? Clare! You have hurt your eye, my dear. That black patch is rather becoming. Let us be gentle with the mask. It fits, gentlemen, it fits!'

'The mask fits!' shouted everybody dutifully, and we all swung into the next stage, for everything was prepared. The prince's coach, white and gold like his uniform and blazoned with the coat of arms of a hero asleep under the earth with a great tree growing out of his groin, drew up outside the long windows. The successful mask-candidate – they must all be already dressed in white – was to be driven straight to the cathedral where choir and clergy were waiting to marry the happy couple. I was not happy, though I was the stepfather of the bride, and should have been. I knew what Edwina had done. At the thought of it my hands began to shake again.

The footman sprang down from the coach, opened the door and pulled down the step. The prince handed his bridal octoroon in and sat her down, her skirts almost filling the seat. I thought it was a poor show, our Clare did not move like a wet dream. The prince knew it but, providing all the forms were followed, he would grit his teeth and go through with it, gallant fellow. I suppose he was short of money like the rest; short of my money; Ash's money. He sat down opposite the mask, lent forward and rapped it playfully. He might have been saying that it was to be like the bridal veil, to be lifted for the first married kiss after the wedding. Then he looked concerned and took out a big lacy handkerchief. He leant forward and began to wipe Clare's eyes. She seemed to be weeping. Then he gave a howl of rage and held up his handkerchief. It was a mass of blood. He snatched off the mask. Blood sprayed over the interior of the coach and over Clare's dress. She collapsed whimpering with pain but the prince took no notice. He flung the door open and with his back turned to us quickly unharnessed one of the white horses, sprang on it and rode fast out of my grounds.

'Damn and blast!' we said in unison, again.

The prince's furious egress had disturbed the doves. Their cooing sounded like '*Blood, blood*'.

It was clear that the surgeon–barber's cautery had not done its work. That, and the emotion of the moment, had made Clare weep blood at her wedding. The imposture was evident; the mask only fitted because she lacked an eye. I knew the prince was entitled to his rage, but could he afford it? I gave instructions for his durbar to open at the usual time the next morning, and sure enough he was there. Those doves were a nuisance. I will see they are shot. '*Blood, blood*' they go.

Dowsabell's first in the queue. It is the mulatto mask today. What trick has Edwina played on her second daughter? Dowsabell – why, I'm proud of her – has got her shoulders back and her Wellingtonian nose well forward. If you weren't looking for it you wouldn't notice the cunningly painted *trompe-l'oeil* on her left eyelid, which conceals an empty socket. The mulatto mask's resonant projections, like the octoroon's, just slip into that socket, I suppose. Dowsabell kneels and bows her head into the mask the prince is holding on his lap. I see that her shoulders shudder as she presses her face into it. She raises her head.

'The mask fits!'

But does it? He leans forward to adjust the tawny face on his bride and it comes away in his hand. Blood spills on his knees. He gets up and looks at me. There is an oubliette in his stare. Then he leaves by the long windows and I hear hooves on gravel where the doves are strutting. Then their '*Blood, blood*' mixes with 'Damn and blast' and I know I must take some action before my prince returns, otherwise my house and wealth will be commandeered and I shall be lodged for my punishment secretly in the lowest sump of its drains, to be shat on for as long as I may live. Sewers are the best dungeons. So I turn on Edwina.

'Yes, this is your work, Madame. You had their eyes removed. Now you've got two one-eyed daughters and they'll be lucky if Lieutenant Whatsit and Reverend Who will have them for chambermaids. Because this is where your scheming has got you, it is you who deserve to be blind, Madame. I think you are already deeply blind, to do such things to your own flesh. I will punish you for my pleasure and to divert His Highness's anger. You will be bricked up in your own boudoir with no food and a little water and when you are hungry the price of a crust will be an eye, Madame, an eye which you will pluck with your own nails out of your own head to buy food.'

Then a voice spoke out of the air.

'Be gentle!' it said.

I looked around. There was nobody. Just the stunned face of

Edwina and the others. She no longer looked like stone but she was giving off misericord perfume and I almost felt sorry for her. It was my real wife's voice in the air, but it seemed to be pleading for Edwina.

'What's this?' I cried. 'Are you calling up the dead to protect you now? Is the Christian gentlewoman a necromancer after all? Is the genteel planner of cathedrals a filthy witch?' Edwina's face crumpled, as though the stone face and cathedral project had been painted on still curtains merely, and the window had been opened, and they were blowing in the fresh breeze. Then I felt a touch on my arm.

'I am here, Father. Oh, let me take that tablecloth, and put it round my shoulders. Can you see me now?'

'There you are, Ash. I wondered where you had got to. I didn't see you standing there. We've had such excitement in the last few days! I've just been telling your mother how we shall finish up the festivities.'

'Yes, Father, I heard. I want you to pardon her.'

'I don't think I can. The prince will expect some punishment to be meted for this fiasco. Some satisfaction.'

'He shall have it. Father, I will try on the first and last mask, of the black woman, on condition that you pardon your wedded wife.'

'She has destroyed half the sight of two women!'

'You will not believe this, but they will be able to see with their blind eye. With their good eye they will see the world as it is, and with their blind socket they will be able to see it as it should be. Stepmother, you have created seers with your cruelty. One visible eye for outward sight, one invisible eye for inward sight. Second sight.'

Edwina was recovering some of her poise, unfortunately.

'Seers?' she spat. 'Your instructions are turning them into witches!'

'As you say, Stepmother. Now I will put on the black mask.'

And it was she! The black woman, moving as she moved, her tablecloth contriving a good approximation of a *chador*. My thoughts were echoed by another voice coming out of the air, from the long window. Were all the spirits now attending us? I could see nobody, yet he was speaking rapturously in the prince's voice.

'It is she, the black woman, standing among the others.' Invisible knuckles rapped Ash's mask.

'It is you, really you, for you have her perfume, which wears no mask.'

And the black mask floated off Ash's face and I could see she knew her lover, for she reached up to kiss him; and as she clasped him in her arms the naked prince became visible as if she were his garment. Now His Highness insisted that we should all dance. I knew I was out of the wood. Moreover that we should all take our clothes off and dance skyclad. I was willing. It was better than eating turd in the oubliette.

'We will dance to the old cathedral where we were to be married . . .'

'Nobody will see us, Highness.'

'Oh yes they will. Then we shall dance on and get married under the great grandmother ash-tree in the centre of the forest.'

'That is a pagan custom, Highness! A witch-wedding.'

'So be it.'

The Rose of Leo Mann

The Rose of Leo Mann

Daughter, bride or flower, which was she?
All three were Rosalie.

John Cobb yawned. It had been a profitable but long day at the trade fair. Lulled by the cultivated tones of his young male secretary Mark Crown, he closed his eyes, relishing the scrupulous leathers and smooth pace of his limousine. He snored. Mark relaxed, looking forward to seeing his girlfriend at the weekend. Max the driver, sensing the inattention of his passengers, put his foot down and went over 100 mph through the dark.

For the past three weeks Mark Crown and his boss had been travelling, visiting head offices, factories, journeying to over a dozen cities for a series of meetings lacking rage, pain or grief, but with much businesslike talk and schedules for signature. 'The product sells itself, Mark,' John Cobb told his aide a hundred times. Each time Mark shook his head. 'No, Mr C, you've got the touch.' Then Mr Cobb would grin and nod modestly. 'I like meeting them,' he said, 'I like seeing how they lap it up. Everyone likes to be wooed, Mark. The product is a substitute for love.' The boss had the magic touch, thought Mark sleepily. Cobb was a salesman to the heart. He had the concentration, the guts, the style. His handsome if foxy looks, his well-above-average height, his good humour, his melodious voice and musicianly hands charmed everyone, and not for the first time the young man considered throwing Mary over and trying his chance with one of Cobb's daughters, not those two talkative beanpoles, no, he fancied the youngest, the pretty but serious one. He dozed and dreamed.

John Cobb shook him. 'Mark. Here we are. The hotel.'

John Cobb puffed on a big cigar. Clouds of pungent smoke turbaned his large head.

'Ish too late to gotobed . . .' John Cobb's voice was slurred. The two men guffawed. They'd had a few, him and Mark. They were the only drinkers left in the bar. It was past one but their loud boozy voices still rose and fell. The barman slouched and yawned mutinously in the shadows, but sprang to his feet and began polishing a glass as the dinner-suited proprietor walked casually into the bar. He stood in whispered conversation with the barman for a moment, looking at the two beery travellers sitting in easy friendship, their collars pulled deeply open, their laughter full of the exhausting fellowship that men drink to find at the end of the day. Then he moved lightly over to their table.

He was a fit, elegantly turned-out, leonine, old-young man. He faced the two men. His expression was a mask of hospitality.

He smiled, introducing himself.

'I'm Leo Mann, your host.'

'Welcome, welcome.' John waved an arm wildly. 'Join us, won't you?'

With an accepting shrug, Leo swivelled a chair round and sat astride it, his fingers curled tightly round the backrest.

Outside the night was clear and cold. The stars shone, trying out new constellations: the clenched fist, the nettle, the castle of twigs, the silver coin, the elephant, the flea, the tree of children. A girl hurrying home looked up at their bright brinks, acknowledging her fears, then ran up the path, unlocked her door and slipped inside to safety.

John sniggered '. . . and she tasted of custard for a week!' The landlord gave a snarl of bored laughter. Leo Mann had heard it all before. He looked at John narrowly. John winked back. 'Good one, eh?' he spluttered. Leo nodded, and looked round restlessly. Mark giggled, hiccuped twice, went limp, and slid in a beautiful relaxation to the floor. John peered down, nudging Leo. The landlord flinched. He didn't like being touched. John didn't notice. 'He's a good lad,' he said tearfully, 'one of the best.'

'One of the best,' Leo agreed dismissively.

'I thought I'd be happy when I was rich,' said John, pouring whisky down his throat, 'yes, son, when I had shabby clothes and worn shoes, I thought a fine suit and a big house would make me happy. But they don't, you know. Last night I had this dream, right? In my dream a double rainbow arched over the sky and made a rainbow bridge and over this bridge my favourite daughter Rosalie ran naked and perfect towards me, her arms held out to me – then I was happy. God, that was happiness . . . But I woke up, Leo, and the daylight fucked me up . . .' John sobbed, drunk as a lord, and put his head down on the table.

Groaning, Mark got up. Leo clicked his fingers and the barman hurried forward obediently, hooking his arms under John's armpits, heaving him up. Mark staggered after them.

Leo sat very still, eyes half-closed, head tilted slightly, as if listening. The light was glossy on his fine white cuffs, on the sheen of his black sleeves. Suddenly he shot out a hand, gnawed ravenously at a leftover beef sandwich.

After a hot shower and a breakfast of aspirin and black coffee, John stepped outside, turning up his coat collar. Everywhere was fresh and sweet to him despite his hangover. In the hour before dawn, a heavy fall of snow had transformed the world. Everything looked different. Bright midwinter sun and the white blaze of snow. He walked over the snow carefully, his footprints altering the whiteness. Last night he had dreamed again of Rosalie. She was a battlemaid riding the whirlwind; on her black horse she came riding, whirling her axe above her head. She was the battlemaid come to kill, offering no kind word, claiming no love. In his dream John fled from her. There was no escape. He heard the thud of the axe on his skull. He felt nothing as he fell into blackness but he heard Rosalie's triumphant laugh and that caused him the most dreadful pain. Spurring her horse she leapt into the next day. John shuddered.

'Chilly, isn't it, sir?'

John frowned. 'You look rough, Mark. Did you sleep in your clothes?'

'Sorry, sir.'

John sighed. His uncharacteristic moodiness puzzled his deputy.

'Mark, what have I forgotten?'

'I don't know, sir, what have you forgotten?'

'Not a joke, Mark.' (A mild rebuke.)

'Ah.'

'What have I forgotten?'

Mark gaped. The clear blue sky was no help.

'Come on, man. It's your job to tell me these things.'

Mark stamped his cold feet and said, 'Well, Mr Cobb . . .'

His boss snapped his gloved fingers impatiently. The wind sighed in the snowladen trees. Quilts and sheets of snow slipped to the ground. Suddenly Mark smiled.

'Your daughter's rose, sir.'

John clapped him on the shoulder.

'Good man. Rosalie's rose. She asked me to bring her back a rose. A rose was all she wanted. But damn it, look . . . it's all snow . . .'

'Over here, sir.' Mark waved. He'd found a grotto hidden behind a high holly hedge. Here John saw what he wanted and, approaching with the confident stride of a rich man, he plucked the single rose blooming in the snow, a deep red rose in full bloom, with dark green leaves; he breathed in its perfume (almond, velvet, a smell of music, a snatched kiss of earth) and shuddered at its boldness, remembering a room long ago swaying like a hammock.

'I'm sure our host won't object.'

A hand gripped John's shoulder hard, forcing him to turn. Breath gusted in his face, not sweet, but rank, animal; a wordless snarl hot in his ear shocked him.

A good two inches shorter than John Cobb, Leo adopted an aggressive stance. His face was whitish and strained, his unshaven jaw tense and set, his eyes curiously unfocused, as if he was stoned; his breathing was fast and shallow. A trail of saliva ran down his chin. Resenting all this, John brushed off Leo's hand and laughed thickly.

'My rose.' Leo confronted him, hunching his shoulders and clenching his fists. His unbrushed hair (about which he was normally quite vain) stood out in corkscrews from his scalp, each hair seemingly charged-up by the electricity of his rage.

'Take it easy. It's just a rose, my friend.'

Leo shook his golden head angrily at John's bluster, yet watched him most attentively.

'I'll pay your price.'

Leo leapt back in fury. He paced twice round the two men, alarming Mark and amusing John.

'I said, I'll pay your price,' John repeated, his voice steady.

Leo blinked his green eyes. Now his gaze was clear and hostile.

'Will you?' He smiled and then shrugged elegantly, cruelly. Mark began to be very frightened.

'Come on, Mann, name your price,' John bullied. He gave the rose to Mark and squared up to Leo.

'Are you sure?'

For answer John took out his cheque book and flourished it under Leo's nose. Mark stammered, 'But don't you think . . .'

Leo turned to stare at the rose in Mark's hand. The flower at once seemed to grow heavy, dragging Mark's arm down; the petals were solid, made of iron, surely, the stem an iron rod, colder than ice. Mark's hand ached terribly, his arm was going numb, dead. Leo stared at Mark hungrily. Mark did not at all like the look in those narrowed eyes, greeny-gold-flecked, with the sense of something waiting to spring forward, a teeth-in-your-throat look. He was sweating and felt bad and knew the stolen rose was to blame for everything. He shivered. Was it just his hangover giving him these dreadful thoughts?

The three men in the snow each feared a different thing.

'How shall I make out the cheque, my friend?' John's bravado was not worthy of his honourable character, but he was in a tough spot.

Leo hummed a waltz tune in a low harsh tone, turning his head from side to side in a deliberate and threatening manner that whittled away the last of Mark's nerve. The boy turned and ran, dropping the rose in the snow.

Leo swooped on it before John could think. He cradled it delicately.

'It's just a rose, man. How much?'

'No money,' the other spat back.

An icy wind blew in their faces. The blue winter sky streamed high and uncaring above them. John knew anything he said now would be a slip of the tongue. He'd bargained all his life. He knew the ropes. Leo spoke menacingly.

'I love my rose.'

'It is the most beautiful, the most excellent rose, my friend. I want this rose for my daughter.'

Leo stepped back and inclined his head.

'My price is the first living creature you meet when you get home. Send me that creature.'

'Nay, lad,' laughed John Cobb, 'be serious.'

Leo licked his lips. He lifted his right hand and stroked John's cheek. John stared back, too surprised to move or speak.

'Think again,' Leo whispered, 'eh?' He tilted his head, sinister yet flirtatious. He looked almost girlish for a moment. The two men stood in silence, almost embracing, almost struggling, yet not touching.

John was not used to giving in. But when he looked into the eyes of his adversary he felt old; he wanted to go home; he'd had enough.

'You sod,' he said.

With a slight bow Leo offered John the rose.

The two men parted grimly. The birds in the garden sang from necessity, even in a changed world.

'He was one hell of a practical joker, Mr Cobb!'

John didn't answer. He looked at the rose. He'd paid a high price for it. No one had bested him for years. But he had what his daughter wanted; a rose. His humiliation was gradually forgotten in thoughts of Rosalie, and as they drove down the motorway he sang:

> 'O my love's like a red, red rose
> That's newly sprung in June . . .'

'No! No!'

Rosalie's cries brought her sisters running.

'Wake up, Rosalie!'

'Rosalie, you're dreaming.'

Rosalie jumped out of bed. Her yawning sisters in their long white pastiche nightgowns looked at her inquisitively. Charlene was sympathetic, Jolene haughty and cross.

Rosalie trembled. In the mirror her sisters were rich and she was poor. She stared down at her tumbled bed.

'What is it, Rosalie?' Jolene came closer, her face eager, sensing vulnerability.

'You were shouting so loud.' Charlene took her arm, led her to the rocking chair.

'I dreamed.'

The sisters nodded, serious as they had ever been in their lives. They asked no more questions, for once doing the right thing, even Jolene.

'I dreamed a lion raped me.' Rosalie looked up at her sisters tearfully.

The girls blinked and stared at Rosalie, then burst into whoops of laughter.

'A lion, a lion . . .' screamed Jolene.

'Pull the other one,' giggled Charlene.

'No, listen,' she begged, 'it was an awful dream . . .'

'I wouldn't mind it, would you?' Jolene nudged Charlene.

'You would mind, Charlene,' Rosalie whined. 'He was so heavy.'

'So heavy, so heavy,' the girls mocked.

'Listen! And he hurt me . . .' Rosalie pulled up her nightgown. 'See, I'm bleeding.'

'Don't be silly, Rosalie, it's just your period,' Charlene snapped. 'Where's your Tampax? I'm going back to bed.'

The sisters flounced out of the room.

Rosalie curled up in the old chair, weeping, afraid of the blood that would not be kept waiting.

From the frosty yard, John Cobb looked up at his sleeping house, the closed curtains of early morning, the latched and solid door, the roof's delicate steep slope, the mullioned windows imitative of grander days; aided by the sight of his fine house, he stepped forward and –

Rosalie opened the door, smiling, beaming.

John did not groan or protest. He had known it would happen like this. He hugged his daughter.

Everyone else in the house slept on. John and Rosalie sat talking quietly in the kitchen. With a bashful, almost guilty smile, John handed her the rose, mortal and fullblown. She held the rose carefully, looking at it with innocent greed.

'It's beautiful,' she said, 'but how did you get such a rose in wintertime?'

'Easy when you know how,' he said dismissively.

'Was it expensive?'

'Pint of Guinness and a packet of crisps,' he said. 'Do you really like it, Rosalie?'

How her mother Cora and her skinny sisters cried on the morning of Rosalie's departure. They said, 'Suppose we never see you again?' She laughed impatiently. She was dressed in her best clothes and looked lovely. The three letters which Leo Mann had written her were stashed in her suitcase. She longed to be off.

'You'll see me again, Mother. Don't be silly. I have to go. Father says I must.'

John Cobb nodded, swallowing hard. It was a bright blowy spring morning. Thinning cloud raced across the sky.

Rosalie fastened her safety belt and, with a last wave to her mother and sisters and a friendly wink to her dad, drove away. Her weeping sisters seeing her go were surprised by a sudden shared pang of jealousy. Weighed down by their father's gifts of diamonds and pearls, they sighed.

It was early evening when Rosalie drew up at the hotel. Her journey had been uneventful, the hand-drawn map easy to follow.

Stroking the brocade-buttoned bodice of her dress straight, she climbed the stairs that led to the private penthouse and walked through the door and into the arms of her correspondent, a strong handsome young man. She fell in love at first sight. His lips, his arms, his smell. 'Rosalie,' he whispered. It was as if they had been longing to meet for years; as if a hostile force had separated them. It was like finding long-lost treasure for both of them. His golden hair and long fair eyelashes complemented her dark hair and white skin. Her buttons flew undone and her nakedness was like a splendid costly garment that only she was permitted to wear. His tongue touched hers. His tongue touched her breasts. His nakedness was honest, lyrical, admirable. He whispered adorable things to her; she gasped. Between the cool sheets of his bed, they burnt and blazed; then slept.

In the morning, she woke alone. She sighed and smiled and stretched. The bedroom was large and luxurious. Through a half-open door she glimpsed a sunken bath with bronze taps. 'Leo?' There was no answer. The canopied bed had sheets and pillows of deep dulled-gold satin. The blinds were still down over the windows. Tempting fortune, she lay back on the pillows, remembering the pleasures of the night.

Suddenly she wrinkled her nose. There was a strange, pungent and not really pleasant smell in the room. Discreetly she sniffed her armpits. No, it wasn't her. Nevertheless, she got out of bed and took a bath. The perfumed bathsalts hid the nasty odour.

Where was her beloved?

She lay in the big bath thinking of Leo's noble letters, of his sensitive touch, waiting for him to return.

But he did not arrive.

Wrapping his yellow towelling bathrobe around her, she went back into the bedroom. Her clothes from last night were still on the floor. She smiled. But, picking them up, she found them cut to shreds as if by sharp scissors. A thrill of horror went through her. She dropped the violated garments and looked round the room, at the heavy but graceful furniture, the gorgeous bed, the simple-hearted landscape paintings on the walls. She caught her breath sharply; the sour, decaying aroma was back. Rosalie looked down at her murdered dress. Her fear turned to anger. She opened her suitcase, found her dullest, ugliest frock and dressed quickly. She was going home.

The door opened. Leo stood on the threshold. He pushed her roughly across the room.

'Good morning to you too,' drawled Rosalie.

Without answering, Leo hit her a tremendous blow across the face. Blood filled her mouth. She fell, knocking her head. She went out cold, seeing stars.

When she came to, he'd gone again. Their bed was ripped apart, just as her clothes had been. Her lips were swollen and split, she ached all over, her left eye was closing up, she had a terrible headache.

The penthouse had a beautiful view over the hotel grounds and the far mountains. How well Rosalie got to know that view, the changing light and shadow over the snowy summits, the stormclouds and the clear weather. It was a hard sight for one not given to indolence.

She spent every single day locked in the apartment. This was for her own safety. She was and was not a prisoner. She had the key; she locked the door; each night at dusk she welcomed Leo with a wife's affection. Each morning, just before dawn, she woke him and sent him out, locking the door behind him. For the past six months she'd lived like this, both happy and unhappy. But everyone has a price to pay for their happiness, she wrote to Charlene.

During that first week Leo had made love to her like an angel every night; every morning he had beaten her. But on the seventh morning Rosalie was ready; she had been training in secret; she dodged his fist. Darting forward she kneed him smartly; while he gasped for breath she bashed him over the head with her shoe and while he was still woozy she tied him up and left him to stew for a couple of hours while she went out shopping. On her return she was pleased to hear him address her in a polite and respectful manner.

'That's all very well, Leo, but what is it you can't help? It had better be good. If it isn't, I'm off.'

'Untie me first, Rosalie.'

'Certainly not.'

She looked down severely at him, wrinkling her nose at the faint constant reek that haunted the apartment, which no plumber could fix.

Leo looked the very picture of shame. His fine stylish tailormade suit was crumpled, his elegance vanished. His shifty gaze flicked round the room.

'Tell me what the trouble is,' said Rosalie gently, crouching down, but not too close to Leo.

He looked at her. He wept. Tears streamed down his face. He looked very young. Now he was tied up, Rosalie re-experienced all her first delight in him.

'I loved a woman three years ago. She was called Opalle-Dragonne. She was wild and wise, I thought. I loved her. But her wildness and her wisdom grew bizarre, unpredictable. I fell out of love with her, and suggested we go our separate ways. Oh how angry she was. How she cursed me. "A man by night, Leo, but a beast by day. Listen to what I say. A man by night but a beast by day. No woman will love you if I can't. A lion by name and now lion by nature; beast; killer; you'll smell of it and live by it." That is what happened to me, Rosalie. I left all my old friends and came here to run this hotel. I didn't want any of them to know what I'd become. No woman was safe with me.'

Rosalie frowned.

'Is all this true?'

'Yes. Every day, when I am running this hotel and looking like a man, I know I am really a lion, and I pad up here and hurt you. I had to trick you here, so that my nature could express itself. I'm sorry.'

He sobbed again.

Rosalie patted his shoulder but he wriggled and snarled and his jaws almost closed on her hand as she jumped back.

'You see, you see,' he wailed, 'you see what I'm like! I'm sorry, I'm sorry!'

Rosalie glared at him. 'Can't you resist this . . . spell?'

'I resist all I can. Often I think, oh the spell has worn off, I am a man. Then the lion-feeling comes back, I enjoy having my big claws and sharp fangs, I can roar, and as for my heavy pelt, oh I'm proud of it, Rosalie.'

'I see.'

'I have to be so careful with the guests. I can't roar at them. I snarl at my staff, no one works here for long. It is such a strain. The barmaids look and smell so delicious but I daren't . . . The police would . . . And I'm good at running a hotel, despite the turnover of staff . . . In a way it's been a great career move, I like it much better than working in the city.'

'A man by night but a beast by day,' Rosalie murmured.

'Yes.'

'You are OK at night?'

'No problem.'

Rosalie sat cross-legged, at a safe distance from Leo, and tried to think. There must be an answer.

'Rosalie,' the lion-man whimpered.

'Yes?'

'I love you, Rosalie.'

'I love you, Leo. You are my blessèd beast.'

The lovers who dared not touch blew kisses across the distance between them. Then Leo's face changed and he roared, he roared and wrenched at his bonds.

'Hush, my love,' called Rosalie. 'Hush, and let me think.'

Obeying Rosalie's instructions, Leo gave her the key. Every day, before dawn, he left and she shut herself in the apartment. He visited only at night when he was a man.

Leo adapted one of the storerooms in the hotel basement to serve as a lion-space. Here behind a locked door he could tear up supplies of cushions and clothes and eat the raw meat he craved. Rosalie drew up a timetable for him, with certain times set aside for him to indulge his lionhood; trying to control the obsession may help, she said. Revel in your lionishness, she told him; Opalle-Dragonne could not have cursed you unless you already had lion in you. Lions have quick reflexes, they have a marvellous sense of smell, of hearing, of the hunt, of weather and of sleep. These skills can help you in everyday life, Leo.

So at set intervals Leo tried to enjoy being a lion. He walked with a loose powerful animal stride. He relished his enhanced senses. (He could mark any drug-carrying guests as soon as they drove in his gates.) Gradually he felt less shackled to the violence of the beast and more in tune with its animal soul. Once they tried to meet in the daytime but the experiment failed, it was too soon. Poor Leo bit Rosalie savagely on the leg and she banned him again. They met at night; and that was their life.

But the days alone were long for Rosalie. She watched the mountains as if interpreting her life by their contraries of shade and light. She grew thin. When the invitation to Charlene's wedding came, she said to Leo, 'I'm going. Remember your lion exercises. Try to be good.'

In Rosalie's absence Leo regressed and did many forbidden things. Several neighbourhood pet rabbits vanished. He watched a new waitress with lordly lust, persuading her upstairs after her shift. She giggled and shrieked in his rough embrace, calling him a beast. 'Look,' she said afterwards, quite angry. 'Teethmarks everywhere, Mr Mann!'
    'You are so delicious,' he growled.
    With a shrug, she put on her torn blouse, her ripped black skirt. 'Just because you're the boss,' she grumbled.
    When night came, he wept, ashamed.
    But each day he paced his territory in the folly and joy of his beasthood, proud and suave, admired by his guests, who suspected nothing; the secret of his charm was hidden from them.
    Still only the nights were safe.

Rosalie shook her head. 'I almost envy Charlene her footballer husband,' she scolded. 'What I have to put up with.' She tossed the newspapers at Leo. 'GIRL BITTEN IN SAVAGE BEAST-MAN ATTACK!' 'THE BEAST STRIKES AGAIN!' 'HORROR OF THE AFTERNOON MAULER!' '"HE ROARED LIKE A LION," SAYS GIRL TRAFFIC WARDEN!'
    Leo knelt on the headlines and threw his arms round Rosalie's waist.
    'I tried, Rosalie, but it is so hard. I am a lion by day. It is deep in my nature now.'
    'Nonsense. You'll be a man day and night soon.'
    'No, no,' he moaned.
    She patted his head tenderly.
    'Yes, Leo, you'll do it.'
    'I should be shot.'
    'Don't say that.'

'Why not? It's what you do to killer animals.'

'You haven't killed anyone.'

'I did, almost.' A hint of pride, but Rosalie frowned reprovingly.

'Anyway,' she said briskly, 'when Jolene gets married, you're coming with me, buster.'

The Doves of Peace were making a humungous noise. The marquee shook and the laser lights swung like djinn fingers over the dancers. The amplified shout-singing of the youths in the band was a metallic and relentless unison; backed up by guitars, drums, a high-pitched ghostly electric samisen and a synthesised balalaika, the band was living up to its reputation as the loudest around. Wedding guests were dancing, lip-reading, smooching, cowering and giggling in the shadows, eating, devouring, pecking, nibbling (compôte, fritters, cake, salami, goulash, sausage); drinking, swigging, swilling, tippling (wine, champagne, beer, vodka and punch). The party was going like a dream, with everyone beautifully dressed and emotional, their faces rainbowed by the tingle and splat of the lights. John Cobb lifted his glass and chuckled.

'AAAAAEYEEEA GAGAGAHAHAHAHA AND SHE CAN!' the lead singer yelled. He was a close-cropped skeletonised boy clad in frayed designer tat, his left cheek tattooed with a dove.

'SHE CAN SHE CAN GAGAGAHAHAHAHA AAAAAA-EYEEEAA,' wailed the ensemble, in their bereaved garments, in their star plumes.

A final blare of gibberish and a long drawn-out orgiastic howl ended the set; the band slumped forward in acknowledgment of their musicianship; the dancers, released from the swagger of noise, began talking, arguing, making arrangements for later. Jolene, looking angelic, floated from group to group, her bride's horseplay exciting everyone, goosing the young men and then bumping bottoms with them, flicking ice-cream at her squealing bridesmaids, riding piggy-back on the obliging shoulders of the best man.

'She's very happy,' said Rosalie.

John Cobb nodded. 'Are you?'

'I guess so, Dad.' She looked fondly across the crowd to where Leo was in serious conversation with a black leather-coated Dove.

'Rosalie!' Dressed like a barbarian Cinderella, Charlene dragged her sister out into the cool dark garden. 'Listen. I have to tell you. I'm pregnant!'

The sisters laughed and sobbed and cuddled and jumped up and
down.

'Your turn soon, Rosalie.'

'Maybe,' Rosalie stammered.

'Where's your father?' Cora Cobb pounced on her daughters. She
was in a rage. 'Where's that new husband of Jolene's? And Rosalie,
your boyfriend' (waspish sneer), 'Leo, is making a right girl's blouse
of himself trying to play guitar with those Dove men. Come on, both
of you, back in here and help me with this so-called party. Charlene,
get your sister and make her put on her going-away dress before she
does something really silly. My god, doesn't she want to start her
honeymoon? And, Rosalie, go and talk to your aunts; they're drinking
too much as usual – !'

Rosalie woke up elated. The night had ended passionately for her and
Leo. But from downstairs a woman's peculiarly deep and rasping
scream got Rosalie up and running. What a scream, from the very
bone of the jaw, from the root of the tongue. Mother!

Rosalie shot downstairs shouting, 'Mother, Mother,' followed by
her yelling aunts.

Flinging herself on Leo, she grabbed him by his mane of hair and
tugged. He elbowed her away hard across the floor and went on
worrying at Rosalie's mother, whose quivering body he had pinned to
the hall carpet. Crouching on hands and knees above her, he nipped
her all over with his teeth, not drawing blood, but scaring her dread-
fully. She flapped helpless hands at him. 'Leo, Leo,' sobbed Rosalie,
crawling towards him.

Suddenly, with a great and almost oriental Ha! of rage, her father
made his entrance. Gripping Leo in a backtwist, he shook him like a
dog, calling for help. His son-in-law Barry helped him drag Leo
roaring to his room. Through the locked door John Cobb threatened
Leo with criminal prosecution. Rosalie did not try to defend Leo. She
sat weeping on the floor. Shame and guilt filled her. Aunt Tulip and
Aunt Jane in a great flutter got Cora upstairs. She was not badly hurt,
but very shocked and confused. Rosalie hated her father for bringing
her the rose. She hated herself for asking for a rose. She hated her
mother for giving birth to her. But she did not hate Leo. Even now
she loved him; she feared losing him, oh never again, one kiss, one
touch. She couldn't bear it.

Yawning, Charlene came downstairs.

'What's all the racket?'

Rosalie, not answering, crawled upstairs to humiliation in her mother's room.

'It's your fault! All of this, your fault! Little bitch!'

'No! It's your fault!' Rosalie blazed at her father. 'You got us into this! You couldn't go to a florist, could you? You had to steal Leo's rose. You had to steal a crazy man's rose!'

'That's enough. Your mother is a sick woman. She has been struck dumb. The doctor says she may never speak again.'

Rosalie sobbed. 'Poor mother.'

John Cobb shook his daughter. 'Listen. You stay home now, Rosalie. You let that sod bugger off. He's bad news.'

Rosalie pushed her father away.

'Where is he? Where is Leo?'

'Him?' her father rapped out. 'Oh, we knocked the piss out of him.'

'Where is he?'

'Stay here with us, Rosalie,' he cajoled. 'He's not worth it. I mean, he tried to eat your mother.'

'He has problems. I admit it. But we're working on them.'

'Working on 'em. Not fast enough, my girl. When stone turns to gold you'll solve that young man's problems. I knew he was a wrong 'un. I knew it.'

'Father, please. Where has Leo gone?'

'Stay here. We all love you. And you'll soon meet some nice guy.'

'Nice guy! Father, I love Leo! Somehow I'll get him free of the spell.'

'Spell? Bollocks!'

'Where is he? Tell me!' Rosalie's voice rang out, terrible and tragic.

Her father smiled spitefully. 'Where is he? Gone with the Doves of Peace. That's where.'

His great laugh wolfed after her as she ran.

'DOVES LEAVE ON WORLD TOUR.'

'FANS OF DOVES FLOCK TO AUSTRALIA.'

'DOVES' FANS GIVEN WHITE FEATHERS AS TOKENS OF LOVE.'

All the tabloids carried the latest gossip about the Doves. Photos of the new guitarist appeared. Rosalie kept all his clippings. In her loneliness her only comfort was that rock bands play by night and sleep by day; perfect camouflage for Leo.

Rosalie bought airline tickets and set off.

The Doves were guarded like royalty or condemned men. Rosalie begged the security guard to let her into the dressing-room or at least deliver her note. 'He's my boyfriend,' she explained. 'That's what they all say. Push off, you stupid cow. And you, and you, and all of you . . .' Shoved back into the crowd of squealing girls, Rosalie yelled, 'Gimme a feather, then.'

She tucked the precious delicate feather into her belt. The crowd in the big amphitheatre roared in the distance, like a great composite beast.

'Leo,' she whimpered.

It was the same story everywhere! Finland, Russia, Canada, Peru, California, New York, Manchester. She couldn't reach him by phone or letter. Was it shame at his attack on her mother or anger with her at not standing up for him on that terrible morning that led to his silence? John Cobb financed her pursuit of Leo, even though a year passed and she never made contact with him, despite following him around the world. As the second year passed, her collection of white feathers took up an entire small suitcase. Then one terrible day she switched on the TV and heard the news: 'Mega rock band Doves of Peace in plane crash in Mexico.'

When she got to Mexico City, Leo had discharged himself from hospital and vanished. Three of the band were dead. The lead singer and the drummer had severe injuries and were in intensive care.

Now, thought Rosalie, no human being can help me.

To cheer Rosalie up, her parents planned a fancy-dress party for her twenty-first birthday. Reluctantly, she gave in to her family's persuasions. Her mother had, against medical expectations, recovered well from her ordeal with Leo. In retrospect she appeared to relish the attack, taking it as some kind of compliment; she was conceited about it and would refer to it at inappropriate moments, at Sunday lunch, or while changing her grandson's nappy. John looked back with some nostalgia to her six months of silence.

Charlene and Rosalie went to the costume shop. They walked along rows of disguises. 'What shall we be, Rosalie? Pig, horse or angel? Queen, burglar, cowgirl, stripper, nurse, soldier, nun, conjurer, spider-woman? Here's where we can try on some of the other lives we might have lived.'

Rosalie nodded, became interested. She strolled dreamily between the colourful rows of new identities. 'Who shall I be, Charlene?' The dresses were soft and sensuous, with a clean and sexy odour about them. They made an atmosphere of secrets; it trembled around the girls.

'This one, you wear this one.' Charlene thrust a costume at Rosalie; a green tunic and brown satin breeches, a pair of high soft leather boots and a sumptuously ruffled blouse. 'You be Robin Hood.'

Rosalie laughed. 'OK, Charlene, I'll do it.'

'Let's see you in it.'

Rosalie pulled off her shabby skirt and jacket and slipped into the cool close-fitting outfit, donning boots and adjusting hat, frills, and wide silver-buckled belt. 'There,' she said breathlessly, 'how do I look?'

Charlene clapped her hands in approval.

Trevor and Barry, Rosalie's brothers-in-law, sat smartly and unhappily dressed as Holmes and Watson, forced into these roles by their teasing wives. Jolene, got up as an enormous strawberry, her legs stalkily thin and green and with the big red strawberry concealing the seven-month bump of her first pregnancy, grinned at Rosalie. On her head Jolene wore a little green circlet of gauze leaves. Charlene was dressed as a baby, wearing a pink sleeping suit motifed with numerous white rabbits and with its own big integral fluffy slippered feet; round her neck a dummy hung from a pink ribbon and she waved a giant pink rattle; she sat on her Sherlock Holmes-husband's lap and insisted he feed her from a bottle which she produced from a pocket in her suit. Her red-faced husband stuck the teat in her mouth and she sucked realistically.

Slim and romantic in her Robin Hood outfit, Rosalie looked out of the window, saying nothing. It was her birthday but she was still sad. She felt she spent every day and night waiting for what never happened – Leo's return – and so she lived as if in the darkness of roots, while above her swayed and stretched a huge green tree; she'd be safe in its branches if she could climb up, but she could not move without Leo.

In came her parents, big smiles of wonder at their own magnificence on their faces. Rosalie stared, dazzled. She and Jolene cheered in courteous recognition. Holmes stood up, dropping Charlene with a bump. 'By Jove,' said Watson.

John Cobb was dressed as the sun.

Cora Cobb was dressed as the moon.

Oh, their nobility, thought Rosalie, tears coming to her eyes, they have dressed like this for my sake, my celebration.

John Cobb, on his best behaviour, wore a fine false golden beard. His floor-length ducal robes of bright yellow satin proclaimed his solar nature. He wore yellow suede gauntlets and a pair of trainers painted gold. His neck was encircled by Cora's best and heaviest gold chain. His face was gilded with theatrical make-up; his eyebrows glittered, and on his arrival the room became brighter.

His light fell upon his wife, the moon.

Cora was the moon at the full. Her crinoline-skirted, full-bodiced dress was pure white, and it shone. Her long gloves were silver lamé. Pearls glowed forgivingly at her throat. Her matronly corseted shape gained moral strength from her lunar gown, over which she wore a tabard of silver fur. Her long grey hair was loose and glinted with silver.

Father, the sun, said loudly, 'Happy birthday, Rosalie!'

In a high clear witty voice, Mother, the moon, said, 'Happy birthday, Rosalie.'

Rosalie stepped forward, laughing and crying, to kiss her familiar parents.

Her sisters kissed her, her brothers-in-law brushed their cheeks awkwardly against her.

'This may be of use to you.' John reached into a deep golden pocket and handed Rosalie a giftbox of golden cardboard. A lustrous bow ornamented the box. John bent forward and whispered, 'Open this box when you're up shit creek without a paddle, girly. OK?'

'OK, Dad. Thank you.'

Cora smiled like a woman amazed at life and eyed Rosalie graciously. She offered her a silver-enamelled egg in a pouch of silvery satin.

'When you don't know which way to turn for the best, Rosalie, and when you know you're walking on eggs, crack this egg open.'

'I will. It's lovely.'

Her ma grinned.

A silence fell on the family. At a signal from John, the guests rushed in, odd and amazing guests, masked, boasting, bluffing, Japanese ladies, Red Indian chiefs, a pillar box, a kippered herring, a trio of vicars, a Jacobite, a Nell Gwyn, a family dressed as *The Sound of Music*, a fox, several tarts and tramps, a couple done up as Lady Macbeth and Dracula, a young lady personifying Autumn, with masses of velvet leaves sewn on her dark-green body stocking. Her sister Winter followed her in; her long fingernails painted icicle-white. They all gathered round Rosalie and sang, 'Happy birthday to you, Happy birthday to you, Happy birthday dear Rosalie, Happy birthday to you!'

Where is my lion, my dove?

Silence. Rosalie, still dressed as Robin Hood, can't sleep.

On her bedside table, her birthday box and her birthday egg shine in the lamplight.

'Where is he?'

It is hopeless. Where in the world is he? Is he man or lion? Do both powers still struggle in him, for him?

All night she thinks of Leo, of the seven lions of one week.

The Red Sea was Jolene's favourite nightclub. She was a devotee of the place. 'Come with us, Rosalie,' she said.

Rosalie disliked the hot smoky atmosphere and the feeling of erotic fraud that permeated the club. But Jolene pestered her to come and she'd given in. She looked at her gloves with intimate despair. Jolene was dancing with a teenage boy, moving without finesse, but with exuberance. Trevor sat watching her. He leaned across to Rosalie.

'She's a bitch,' he said. He jerked his head in his wife's direction. 'She should be home with the baby.' Rosalie didn't answer. I won't get involved, she thought coldly. She despised Trevor, the way he looked at her with a kind of disdainful lust.

'Dance?' he asked idly.

'No.'

Her brother-in-law shrugged and went over to the bar. Rosalie was fed up. She picked up her jacket and made for the exit. A middle-aged man with a very pale face said something to her. 'What?' she said hazily. He helped her back to her table and sat beside her. He didn't look the chatty type. Jolene danced by them and gave Rosalie the thumbs up.

The man, interpreting the gesture, blushed. He was dressed conservatively, expensively. His hands were big and well cared for; he closed them in fists, nervously, not threateningly.

'Are you the girl who's looking for Leo Mann?' he asked. Rosalie nodded. He looked at her gravely.

'He's upstairs, living with the dancer.'

'Here?'

'Don't say I told you.' He got up.

'Wait . . .' said Rosalie hoarsely. 'Don't go . . .'

As she spoke Jolene slapped her husband across the face and he batted her one back. The dancers scattered and, in the confusion, Rosalie's informant disappeared.

Two days later, in the afternoon, Rosalie walked unhurriedly from the tube station through the narrow streets until she came to The Red Sea club. It was shut up at this time of day, a hutch of a place, with garbage bags stacked outside. A gaudy picture of a big bare-breasted woman parting the Red Sea stared down at Rosalie. Unimpressed, Rosalie crossed the street to a café and ordered a coffee. Ten minutes later she went home thoughtfully.

In the evening she returned to look for Leo. She carried a Sainsbury's carrier bag. In it, wrapped carefully in tissue paper, were her parents' gifts, in case she needed them. Above her head, The Red Sea glowed in scarlet neon. She walked in.

'He's not here.' Thin-lipped, sulky, short-skirted, puffy-eyed, the woman spoke in a monotonous unexpectedly deep voice. Her fiery hair was teased into a mass of snaky curls. 'Not here,' she drawled. Such is my will and command, she might have added. She blew cigarette smoke into Rosalie's face, looking her up and down hard-heartedly. Rosalie submitted to this scrutiny. Liar, she thought. Liar, liar.

'Tomorrow?' she asked.

The woman shrugged. 'No.' She edged Rosalie towards the door.

'Can I use your cloakroom?'

'Down there.' The thin woman pointed, then turned on her hooker's heels and went to have a good laugh with her inseparable friend out the back.

In the seedy ill-lit toilet, Rosalie threw up. Her head swayed, her courage failed. She wiped her mouth and stared in the mirror. Her sisters and her mother and her father seemed far away. Alone, scared, her hands trembling, she lifted the lid of the golden box her father had given her.

Inside was a dress of gold silk, as fine as goldleaf. She shook it out with a long low whistle of admiration. It fitted her like a second skin. Slashed to the thigh to allow movement, with a plunging bodice and a low back, it was a dress in the vogue of lust. It shimmered like the promise of orgasm after orgasm. In the mirror she saw how she had been transformed, and smiled.

As she wiggled into the dim club, there was a sudden silence. Then one man sighed deeply, appreciating the raised tone, and other men whispered, 'Heavens and earth', 'Well I'm blowed', 'Did you ever?' and 'You don't see many like that', in a chorus of marvelling. The women sat tight on their chairs. Rosalie slithered up on to a bar stool and ordered a rum and blackcurrant. 'There you go, angel.' Rosalie inclined her head pertly at the barman. She sipped her drink. 'Ouch!' A finger and thumb pinched her bare forearm hard.

'Hey.' It was the redhead, staring.

'Watch the fingers,' Rosalie snapped.

'So-*rry*. My name's Opalle-Dragonne. Your dress is great. What do you want for it? After all, baby, it's more me than you, isn't it?'

'Is it?'

'I gotta have it. How much?'

'You want to buy it?'

'She's quick. Yeah. Name your price.'

Rosalie looked at her empty glass.

'Jack!' Opalle ordered fresh drinks.

Rosalie sipped.

'My price isn't money.'

'What then?'

'Flesh and blood.'

'Say again.'

'Flesh and blood. Leo. He's here, isn't he? Let me see him. Then I'll give you the dress.'

Opalle-Dragonne bit her lip. Rosalie got up, slinking the gold dress smooth over her hips.

'OK. Just for half an hour. No more. He's got troubles enough. Have another drink. Come on. You can go up in a bit. I'll tell him you're here.'

'Up there.' Opalle-Dragonne stabbed a scarlet fingernail towards the stairs. She raised her eyebrows as Rosalie swayed up and out of sight.

Leo was sleeping on a sofa. The poky untidy room was too warm.

Leo looked ill, he snored and twitched. His hair was matted and greasy.

She knelt by him, fearing that he would reject her or that her own feelings would turn empty. She touched his shoulder gently, quickly before her thoughts darkened any further. 'Leo, Leo, wake up. My love, wake up.' He groaned and his eyelids flickered but he didn't wake; he breathed slowly and noisily. He stank of booze.

'Leo, wake up!' She shook him, begging him to open his eyes and see her. She tried to lift him but he lolled back on the cushions. She stood up, panting, and realised he was drugged.

'Leo . . .' Loneliness, frustration, misery stunned her. She had been tricked.

'What a sleeping beauty, eh?'

Opalle-Dragonne leaned in the doorway, smiled knowingly. Without answering, Rosalie stripped and stood naked before the other woman.

'Not much to boast of, are you?' Opalle-Dragonne commented.

Still in silence, Rosalie flung the gold dress at the other woman's feet. In exchange Opalle tossed Rosalie's jeans and jumper across the room. On Opalle the gold dress was despotic, insectile, peculiar, seductive. She glanced at herself in the mirror, impressing even herself. Rosalie welcomed her old clothes back, she was comfortable in them. Both women looked at Leo.

'Clear off!' Opalle-Dragonne gave her a push.

Rosalie blushed and ran downstairs, planning her next move.

When Leo woke Opalle-Dragonne was singing a song about fire in her rough husky voice. His head ached. Her song hurt. 'Is it day or night?' he asked.

'Daytime,' she said, and began singing again.

'I must go home.'

'Home, Leo? They hate you there. Rosalie hates you.'

'Who's Rosalie?'

Opalle-Dragonne looked pleased but did not answer.

'Only with me can you be safe, Leo. Only with me. I made you a lion. I am the lion-maker and lion-tamer. I am the only woman who is safe with you.'

He snarled at her then and leapt forward but, snatching up her whip, she drove him back. In her gold dress she wielded the lash of her love. He crouched on the floor, covering his head with his arms.

She danced around him. He cowered. 'Rosalie, Rosalie,' he cried. 'Who's Rosalie? Why does that name make me sad?'

Opalle-Dragonne sang harshly, 'Lord Leo, Lord Leo, come to my fire; fire, fire, I am the dragoness, I am your mate, beast to your beast; lion and dragon belong together. By tongue, tooth and nail, I have you, Lord Leo!'

She lay down with him and embraced him, with snaky elbows and gliding slithering limbs; her voice shut him off from the rest of the world.

In the taxi en route to the club Rosalie cracked open the silver egg. She was in a mood of judgment. Certain acts of revenge also trembled in her imagination.

With great care she lifted an ornate silver necklace from the halved egg. It was antique, and a medallion hung from the silver links, depicting a mother hen with twelve chicks, six to the left, six to the right; and all worked in great detail, feather and beak and claw, elaborate yet realistic. She fastened the silver necklace around her neck easily, accepting its aura of privilege and domesticity. She relaxed, and her nature settled into a further poise.

The barman greeted her with an astonished shake of his head. Ice in her Coke, *and* a slice of lemon? Three men at the other end of the bar gave her the once-over and laughed without sweetness but the entrance of Opalle-Dragonne in her golden gown quelled them to a mutter. She slid on to the stool beside Rosalie and her fingers went straight to the necklace, stroking the hen and chicks; her eyes shone and her mouth curved greedily.

'Back again,' she said roughly.

'Back again,' the girl answered.

'How much for your necklace, Rosalie, silly Rosalie?'

'As before, Opalle-Dragonne. Flesh and blood.'

'As before, Rosalie. It's a deal.'

Rosalie looked down at Leo. She knew her strength. Taking him by one arm, she hefted him off the low couch and threw him over her shoulder in a fireman's lift. The taxi was waiting in the alley. If she could get him down the stairs. Gasping, grunting under his comatose weight, Rosalie tottered to the door. But Opalle-Dragonne was there, shaking with silent laughter. Rosalie teetered, letting Leo slip back on to the couch. Opalle-Dragonne stopped laughing.

'How dare you?' She spoke incredulously. Rosalie stood silent, hands on hips.

'Don't you want my necklace then, Opalle-Dragonne?' Tauntingly, Rosalie fingered the silver chain.

'Give it to me!'

Rosalie fastened the necklace around her rival's neck. The two women, face to face, breathed in each other's breath. Opalle-Dragonne's skin was lightly freckled, Rosalie's was paper-white. She was giving away the second of her birthday gifts. 'There,' she said, her voice breaking, 'may you wear it always.'

'I am glad you are being sensible,' said Opalle-Dragonne, 'and that . . .' Suddenly she shuddered and put a hand to her mouth.

'What is it?'

Opalle-Dragonne shook all over and her face sharpened in pain. 'Oh, oh,' she moaned.

'What is it?' Rosalie was frightened.

Opalle-Dragonne clutched and overturned a small table as she fell to her knees. 'Heavy,' she gasped, 'it's too heavy. Take it off.' She clawed at the necklace, sweating, groaning under its weight.

Rosalie bent forward and slid her fingers underneath the wings of the mother hen. The silver was as light as a feather.

'There's nothing wrong. Get up, Opalle.'

The other woman swore. 'I can't, stupid. It's too fucking heavy!' Opalle-Dragonne arched her back. 'Oh Jesus, take it off, Rosalie!'

'There's nothing wrong.' Rosalie frowned and walked round the struggling woman. Opalle's head bent slowly to the floor as the necklace dragged her down. With a sob she tore at her dress now. 'The dress! It's too tight, it's crushing me! Rosalie, help me!'

Rosalie ran her hand down Opalle's back. 'It's just a dress. A dress can't hurt you, Opalle-Dragonne.'

'It's crushing me! Aargh!'

Opalle crawled round the room in torment. The silver necklace was a millstone, the gold dress a vice.

'Can't breathe, can't breathe,' she croaked.

'That's very odd, Opalle-Dragonne. And very inconvenient. For you, that is. For me, very convenient.'

Rosalie sat on a little spooky chair and watched Opalle-Dragonne writhe and twist on the floor, the necklace and the dress punishing her.

'Help me!'

'You'll survive,' promised Rosalie. Grinning broadly, she got up and slung Leo snugly across her shoulders as if he were a sleeping child and made for the door.

'Help me,' mouthed Opalle-Dragonne, but Rosalie shut the door on the woman collared and pinioned in silver and gold.

She staggered out into the street. The taxi-driver helped her get Leo into the cab.

'As a newt is he, love?'

Rosalie nodded tolerantly.

She sat by his bedside, the two bright halves of the silver egg in her lap. She was tired but happy. Nodding off, she dreamed of her wedding day.

Her father touched her shoulder. He put a cup of tea on the table beside her, and tiptoed silently out. The house was quiet but full of virtues.

She placed the two halves of the shell together but knew she could not mend the silver egg; it had to break and enter the future just like everything else.

At first light Leo opened his eyes.

'Where am I?'

Rosalie looked at him with love and relief.

'Where am I?'

'With Rosalie.'

He said, in amazement, 'I had forgotten you, Rosalie. Who am I, though?'

As if for answer, Rosalie pulled back the curtain. The morning sunlight streamed in, illuminating everything. She stared at him intently. Leo shaded his eyes with his hand. 'Who am I?' he repeated.

Rosalie sat on the edge of the bed.

'You are Leo. You are to be my husband. You are a man. Don't you remember?'

He frowned. 'I dreamed I was a lion.'

Rosalie nodded. 'It was a dream.'

Just as she broke the egg, she can break the spell. She leans forward and kisses him. Leo smiles. He is free. The broad daylight is his.

Flower, daughter or bride, which is she?
All three is Rosalie.

A NOTE ON THE AUTHOR

Peter Redgrove was born in 1932. He was educated at Taunton School, Somerset and at Queens' College, Cambridge, where he was Open and State Scholar in Natural Sciences, and became a founder-member of 'the Group'. From 1954–61 he was a scientific journalist and editor. In 1961 he won a Fulbright Award to travel to the USA as Visiting Poet to Buffalo University, New York. In 1962 he returned to England to become Gregory Fellow in Poetry at Leeds University for three years. After this he freelanced for a year before joining the Falmouth School of Art from 1966–83 in order to teach creative studies. During 1974–5 he was O'Connor Professor of Literature at Colgate University, New York. He is now a freelance writer and has gained a wide reputation in several interlinked fields: as a poet, a novelist, a playwright and in psychological practice. His Grimms' fairy stories were first broadcast on Radio 3 in 1987 and received great critical acclaim. He lives in Cornwall with his partner Penelope Shuttle, who was the co-author of *The Wise Wound*.